FORSAKEN & FORGOTTEN: SATAN'S REALM

DUSTY MCGOWAN

ISBN Number: 979-8-9908073-0-3 (E-book)

ISBN Number: 979-8-9908073-1-0 (Paperback)

LCC Number: 2024911757

Forsaken & Forgotten: Satan's Realm

Edited by: Patricia Kyle

Cover design by: Teleah Moore

Published by:

PO Box 1819, Owings Mills, MD 21117

www.maynetre.com

All Scripture quotations are taken from the King James Version. Used by permission from Cambridge University Press.

"Great Is Thy Faithfulness" by Thomas O. Chisholm, Copyright © 1923 (Public Domain, 2019).

Printed in the United States of America

First Printing 2024

10 9 8 7 6 5 4 3 2 1

ACKNOWLEDGMENTS

I would like to thank God the Father, the Son, and the Holy Spirit for my salvation and this finished work.

Thank you, David, for the use of your laptop, where this story first started to come to life.

Thank you, Sue & Lynn, for your many prayers regarding this book. Thank you for reading the various drafts and giving your feedback with notes on the pages. I listened to most of them, and still have them. Thank you for your encouragement when I'd hit a roadblock, whether it was a computer crash, corrupted file, or a broken printer. Thank you, Lynn, for gifting me your old desktop when mine broke, leaving me with no excuses to finish writing. This book wouldn't be what it is without all of your help.

Thank you, Destiny Carrico, for my author photo.

Thank you, Tara, my darling wife, for telling me about this publisher.

Thank you, Reader, for picking up this book.

PROLOGUE

Among songs and praises, a dark figure strode into the Heavenly courts of the Almighty God.

"Satan," the voice of God said. "From where do you come from now?"

"From preparing my world the way I see fit," Satan replied.

"Whom have you chosen?" asked the Lord.

"As I told You last time, a 17-year-old girl named Jessica White."

"What do you plan to accomplish?"

"To break her, to cause her to renounce You. What about You? Who have You chosen?"

"You may do as you wish to her, except to kill her or hurt her physically. Is that understood?"

"You didn't answer my question."

"Is that understood?"

"Yes... I understand."

"Good, you can see yourself out."

"You didn't tell me who You have chosen."

"You don't need to know at this time."

Grumbling, Satan turned to walk away.

"Oh," God said, "one more thing: Michael will be helping the ones I have chosen."

Ones?! Michael?! "So, all I get to know is that there's Michael and whoever else?"

"Yes."

"Whatever."

Satan stormed out.

CHAPTER ONE

August 2003

"Jess! Jess, wait up!"

Jessica White looked around to see who was calling her. She didn't really need to because she recognized the voice. Timothy Jackson came running up to her.

"Hey, Tim, what's up?" she asked.

"Hey, I was wondering if you wanted to go to Pips? The guys are there."

"Actually, I was already on my way there."

Pips, as they call it, is Pippirelli's Pizza, the local hangout spot for the area kids.

"Oh, yeah, okay," Tim said.

Jess smiled. *I wish he'd just tell me he likes me*, Jess thought. *Of course, you could tell him.*

Tim stood an inch taller than Jess' 5' 1" frame, his freshly shaved head shining in the mid-afternoon sun.

"What happened to all that hair of yours?" Jess had asked when he first started shaving his head.

"Decided to get rid of it," Tim had said. "I wanted something different. Something cooler for the summer."

Jess had laughed at his logic, but he had made sense, in her opinion. She met Tim when she and her mom first moved to town.

Tim, John, Plate, Ashley and Sarah, really...

In the passenger side of their blue minivan, Jessica sits, thinking her life is over, while her mom, Liz, hums to the music of a Country song on the radio.

"It's not fair," Jess mumbles.

"Hmm...?" her mom says, distracted from the radio.

"It's not fair that we have to move away. Away from all my friends."

Turning off the radio, Liz says, "Honey, listen—"

"And what kind of place names their town *Forsaken & Forgotten*? I mean, come on, Mom, don't you think that's a bit... I don't know, hopeless? Depressing?"

"Honey," her mom started again, "I know it's rough on you. Hey, it's rough on me, too. I don't know why Great Aunt Lucy left me her house when she passed on, but it sounds like a great place. Perfect for the both of us. And after careful thought and prayer, I decided it would be best."

"Why did you and dad have to get divorced anyway?" Jess pleaded. "I mean, there weren't any problems when you guys were together. We wouldn't have had to move, either."

Liz sighed. "Sweetheart, there were many problems while we were married. You just didn't know it. We did our best to protect you from all that."

"I miss him."

Liz looked at Jess and said, "I know you do, Hon. But after the divorce, he simply vanished. I don't know where he is."

After a few moments, Jess said, "You never answered my question."

Liz, looked at her. "What question was that?"

"What kind of place names their town Forsaken & Forgotten?"

Liz smiled. "I don't know. Maybe you can get the history of the town when we get there. And if you're still bothered by the name, pray about it. Maybe you'll find peace by the time we get there."

"How much farther is it, anyway?"

"Oh! About thirty minutes. In the meantime, read Job and do a little praying."

"Job? Why Job?"

"Well, with you being so worried and all, I thought you'd like to read that Satan has no power, except what God allows him to have, no matter what."

For the first time during the trip, in a long time really, Jessica smiled.

"I think I'll do that."

"That's a good girl," Liz said. "By the way, the street name is 'Peace.'"

Jess smiled and reached in the back seat and grabbed her Bible and opened the book of Job and began reading and praying.

"Lord, I know you've got a plan, like you did with Job, but I just don't see it. All I see at the moment is a big question mark. I've read Job enough times to know towards the end that not every question that gets asked is answered in the way that's expected, but I do know You, who You are and what You are able to accomplish. I ask that You go with us on this new chapter of our lives. I ask this in Jesus' name. Amen."

Jessica, be of good cheer! You will make friends. I will be with you. You are protected in My hands!

Jessica jumped with a start and looked at the radio, it wasn't on. Then she looked at her mom.

Her mom looked at her.

"Are you okay?" she asked.

"I...I heard a voice, saying...."

"Saying what?" her mom asked, looking worried.

"Well, saying everything will be fine."

Liz smiled.

"See? I told you to put it in God's hands. When you talk, He listens; when you listen, He talks."

"How...how..."

"Do I know it was God?" Her mom finished. "Like I told you I did a lot of thinking and praying about the move, and He answered me, loud and clear!"

"Like what?" Jess asked. She then said in a booming voice, "Elizabeth Jean White! Pack it up and get out of town!"

Liz and Jess both laughed. "Something like that," Liz said. "But not totally."

"I do feel better now. Thanks, Mom."

"No problem, anytime."

After a couple of minutes of silence, Liz turned the radio back on and started singing.

Jessica joined in, also.

"We're here!" Liz announced a few minutes later.

"We are?" Jess asked.

"Uh-oh," Liz said pulling into the driveway.

Five youths were in the driveway, apparently playing basketball.

Three boys and two girls. The kids turned around and stood there. One of them, maybe the oldest walked up to the driver's side door.

Liz rolled the window down a crack.

"Hi, ma'am," he said. "Can I help you?"

"This is my house."

The boy smiled.

"So, you must be Ms. White, right?"

"Yes," she said puzzled. "Do I know you?"

"Oh, no. I knew--well we--" pointing to the others "...knew Miss Lucy, and she told us a lot about you."

"Um...that doesn't explain why you're playing ball in the drive."

"Oh! She said we could. Since she didn't have any kids, she put up the basketball hoop so she could kinda feel like she had some. We were all close to her. Which is why I know who you are."

"That make sense...I guess."

The boy smiled.

"Sometimes, Miss Lucy would invite us over to have lunch with her, and she'd show us pictures of her family and tell us stories. We loved to visit her. She was a great lady."

Liz wiped a tear away. "I think I lived the closest to her. It's a shame I didn't come see her when I could. Thank you for keeping her company."

"It was no problem," he said, smiling. "I'm John, by the way. The short, blond guy is Tim, the other one is Plate, the redhead is Ashley, and the other's Sarah."

The kids waved, Liz and Jess waved back.

"Plate?" Liz asked.

"He'll clean his plate, no matter how much you put in front of him."

Jess laughed.

"Hey, you need help moving in your stuff? We'd be happy to help."

Jess and Liz looked at each other. Liz lifted an eyebrow as if to say, *"See? God supplies."*

Looking back at John, she said, "That would be wonderful. Thanks."

"No problem," John said with a smile.

A couple hours later, Jess stood outside with John, Plate, Tim, Ashley, and Sarah, talking.

"Thanks, guys. I don't think we would've been able to move all our stuff in today without your help."

"Hey," Tim said. "We were in the neighborhood."

Everyone laughed.

"Of course, we were, Tim," Ashley replied, "We live on the same street."

"Yeah," John said, putting Tim in a headlock.

Jess chuckled. "Hey, I almost forgot. Are there any churches close by? I wanna make sure we've got some place to worship this Sunday."

"Yeah," John said, releasing Tim. "It's a couple blocks away. We all go there. Even Miss Lucy went there. Right now, our youth group is really struggling."

"Yeah?" Jess asked. "Why is that?"

"Not many youths and no youth leader," John said. "But we do try to make the best of it. We'll have Sunday School teachers make plans every now and then."

"We are supposed to be getting one soon, though," Tim put in.

"Oh, okay. Cool. That sounds great."

"Jessica!" Liz called from the porch. "Come on, honey, we've got to get some rest. I've got to find a job first thing in the morning."

"I'm coming, Mom!" Jess calls over her shoulder. She then turned to her newfound friends and said, "I gotta go. Good night, guys, and thanks again for all your help!"

"Hey, wait," Sarah said. "Pips is hiring, let your mom know."

"Pips?" Jess asked, turning around.

"Oh," Sarah said, slightly embarrassed. "It's short for Pippirelli's Pizza. Everyone here just calls it Pips."

"Yeah," Tim said. "It used to be just a pizza place, now it's more like a restaurant. It also has arcades and a couple of pool tables."

"Okay, sounds great. I'll see you guys later."

Not even a whole day, and already five friends, Jess thought, as she ran up to the house.

Thank You, Lord...

"Jess? Earth to Jessica?"

"Huh? Oh!"

"I've been talking to you. Where've you been?"

Jess smiled. "Moving day, when I first arrived."

"Ah," Tim said, with a smile. "Good times."

Jess laughed.

A man dressed in all black bumped into Jess, dropping his ice cream.

"Oh! I'm so sorry," Jess said.

The man pulled down his sunglasses, revealing soulless gray-blue eyes.

"You should be," he said, and walked off.

A cold chill went down Jess' spine. She shivered.

"Are you okay?" Tim asked.

"Did...did you see his eyes?"

"No, what about them?"

"They...were soulless... and cold."

Tim looked back at the man then looked back at Jess.

"Come on, let's get inside."

"Okay..." Jess said as they entered Pippirelli's Pizza.

———————

In an abandoned house, just outside of town, there are five youths, four of them gathered around in a circle. They had a lit candle in the circle.

As the teens chant, the flame grows hotter and darker, until, at last, the flame is black.

"Lucifer," one of the teens said. "Our master, hear us this day. Has the time come for your plan?"

From out of the flame, a voice speaks.

"Yes, my servants. The time is now right. You will meet one of my ambassadors in the cemetery just after sundown. There you will be given further instructions. In so doing, you prove your loyalty to me!"

"Yes, my master. Thank you."

From the flame, arose laughter. Demonic laughter.

A gust of wind blew the flame out, leaving an echo of that laughter.

"That's it, then," the teen said, facing the others.

"Trish, do you want me to gather the others and meet you at the cemetery?" One of the boys asked.

"Yes, Travis," Trisha replied. "See to it."

Travis left to gather the rest of The Faithful.

"Aaron, Lloyd," Trisha said. "You two head out to the cemetery and get things ready."

"Yes, ma'am," they said in unison, and left.

Twins, Trisha thought. Always talking together like that.

"What are we gonna do, Trisha?" asked her sister, Kim, who was watching in one corner.

"We, my dear sister, are going home until it is time."

"Oh! Okay."

Kim wasn't sure about all this. All she wanted to do was get closer to her older sister, Trisha.

Trisha, Travis, Aaron and Lloyd were on the council of The

Faithful. Kim didn't know what all they did, but Trisha invited her to come along and watch, and even participate.

"As long as you don't tell Mom," Trisha would say.

"I won't. I promise," Kim would assure her.

As time went on, Kim felt more and more uncomfortable with these meetings.

Today was no exception. Today was the second or third time she had heard the Flame "speak" and it terrified her.

What have I gotten myself into? She'd asked herself. *I guess I'll find out tonight.*

She wasn't sure if she wanted to go, but she would.

For her sister.

CHAPTER TWO

"Tim! Jess! Over here!"

Tim and Jess looked around and spotted John in the corner booth waving them over to join the rest of them.

"Come on guys, Plate's eating everything in sight!"

Tim looked at Jess and said, "Big surprise," with a grin.

"What's up, Cue Ball?" Plate said, finishing his drink.

"Same o', same o'," Tim replied.

Since getting his head shaved, Plate called him different nicknames like, Kojak, Baldy, Cue Ball. None of which he had a problem with. He knew it wasn't mean spirited.

As they took their seats in the booth, Sarah noticed Jess' uneasiness.

"Hey, Jess, are you okay? You look a little pale."

"Did you see the guy dressed in all black leave just before we walked in?" Jess asked.

"Can't say that I did," John said. "I've been watching the door for you guys. Why? What's up?"

"Nothing. Never mind."

"The guy freaked her out after he bumped into her," Tim said.

Ashley touched Jess' hand. "Are you okay?"

"Yeah, I guess. Thanks."

Ashley smiled.

Jess smiled back.

A waitress came to the booth.

"Hey, Julie," Jess said. "Where's Mom?"

"In the back," Julie said with her southern drawl.

"Doing the paperwork and ordering what we need. Do you need me to get her for ya?"

"Uh, no. I haven't seen her today and I wanted to know if she was okay."

Julie smiled. "With her running things here, she's okay and so is the restaurant."

Jess laughed.

"Let me give ya a few more minutes to figure out what y'all want. In the meantime, what'll you have to drink?"

"Water," Jess said.

"Apple juice," Tim replied.

"And a refill for the rest of y'all? Coming up!"

As she walked away, Plate said, "I love her southern accent."

Ashley punched his arm.

"Ouch!" Plate said, pretending to be hurt. "But not as much as I love you, Babe."

"That'll get you nowhere," Ashley replied.

They all laughed.

Plate, whose real name is Paul, adopted his name because he could always finish his plate before anyone else, and still ask for more. He and Ashley had been together since before Jess moved to town. The same went for John and Sarah.

John and Sarah also study martial arts together, they are both on their way to becoming black belts. Plate, on the other hand, says he studies different forms of martial arts on the internet, no one knows if he's really learned anything from it, since he doesn't practice out in the open or anything. Ashley would rather read and practice archery than learn martial arts. Tim likes to play his first-person video games like Metroid and Halo.

Jess just likes to support her friends by going to martial arts practice, doing some archery, or playing a game or two with Tim, but her favorite thing is reading.

"Hey, honey. How's everything?"

Jess' mom, Liz, came walking up to the booth where they were sitting.

"Hey, Mom," Jess said, rising to give her mom a kiss.

"Good. What, did Julie tell you I was here?"

"No," Liz said. "I saw you walk in. The office door was open. I thought I'd take a break and say hi. Hi, guys," Liz said to the rest of the kids at the table.

A volley of greetings shouted from the booth.

Liz laughed. "Well, I better get back to work. I'm gonna be home a little late tonight, Jess. Don't wait up."

"Do I ever?" Jess said with a smile.

"No, but you're up anyway."

Mother and daughter laughed.

"See you later. Love you, Mom."

"Love you, too. Bye guys," Liz said as she went back to work.

Liz was promoted to the Manager of Pips after working there only six months. The owner, Jack Pippirelli, was so impressed with her abilities that he gave her a promotion and a raise just so he wouldn't get to the breaking point.

"Liz," he had said, "you are doing a great job. Would you consider becoming my manager? It hasn't been easy running this place since Ella died, and I could use a little break."

Mrs. Pippirelli died suddenly from a heart attack three months before Liz and Jess moved to town. Jack was still in shape, such good shape, you wouldn't think he was nearing eighty, but with running a restaurant and losing his wife, it was beginning to take a toll.

"I'd be happy too. Thank you for the vote of confidence," she said, smiling.

"No, thank you for helping me."

"Here's your water, apple juice, and your refills."

Julie said, coming back to the booth. "Anything else?"

"I'll have a hamburger, with all the fixings," Jess replied.

"Me, too," Tim said.

"Before you say anything, I'm cutting you off," Ashley told Plate.

Julie chuckled. "Okay, two burgers with everything. I'll be right back with your meal."

While they were waiting for their food, Jack Pippirelli walked up.

"Hey, kids," he said.

"Mr. Pippirelli!" Jess said, standing to give him a hug.

"Happy Birthday! How was your two-week vacation?"

"Short," Jack replied. "And how many times have I told you to just call me Jack?"

Jess blushed.

"Anyway," Jack went on, "it gave me time to rest, see my son, Charlie, my grandson, Jay, and see my beautiful new great grandson, Joe. I have to tell you that Tennessee is beautiful, too. I enjoyed spending my birthday down there with them."

"Honestly, Jack," Sarah said, "you look too good to be a great grandfather."

Jack smiled. "Thanks, Charlie and I got to talking and he wants me to retire and move down there and be with the family. Same thing he said before Ella died."

"But, what about this place?" Jess asked.

"What would you do with it?"

"Now relax, Jess," Jack said. "I said we were talking, not that it was happening. I'd have to talk to your mom about all this before it happened."

Jack bent down and told Jess in a whisper, "Besides, I think your mom would do just fine with this place."

He then winked at her.

"Wha..." Jess started, but Jack put his finger to her lips and with a smile he said, "Shh..."

After standing, Jack said, "If you'll excuse me, I have to let Liz know I'm back. Bye, kids."

As Jack walked off, Tim asked, "Did he just say he was giving your mom the place?"

"You heard?" Jess asked.

"I guess he was the only one," Ashley said.

"Dude, that'd be cool," Plate said.

"Hey, guys," Jess said, "keep it down. It's not official or anything. It's just talk."

"Yeah," John said. "Let's keep it down, we don't want any rumors started because of us."

Everyone agreed to drop the subject.

Wow, Jess thought. *Mom might own the restaurant soon. Hope she can handle it.*

"Here's your two burgers," Julie said, coming back to the booth. "Anything else?"

"No, I think we're good," John said, looking around the booth to make sure.

"Thanks."

Julie smiled. "Be back with the check in a jiffy."

As Julie was turning around, she almost bumped into Jeff, the kids' youth pastor.

"Oh!" Julie said.

"Whoops! Sorry, Julie," Jeff said. "My fault. I gotta remember that the waitresses here are always on the move."

Julie laughed. "That's okay. It's not the first time I've almost ran into someone and I'm sure it won't be the last."

Jeff laughed. "No, I guess you're right."

As Julie left, Jeff watched her with a smile. When he turned his attention back to where it was supposed to be--the five youths--they laughed.

"You did that on purpose, didn't you?" John said.

"Did what?" Jeff asked, innocently.

"You planned to bump into Julie, didn't you?"

"Man!" Plate said. "Just ask her out, will ya?"

"Was I that obvious?"

"Yeah," John said, "you were."

"I'll ask her, when the time is right."

Jeff Jones was twenty-eight when he first became the youth pastor two years ago. Some people thought he was too young. Others just thought the church should forget about having a youth pastor because of the bad experiences they'd had in the past. The last youth pastor, thirty-five-year-old T.J Brooks, turned out to be an abusive drunk.

The youth pastor before T.J., David Spark, was a bit different. He was forty-two and single. He had a doctorate's degree in theology as well as in child psychology. Everyone thought he was perfect, except the children. None of the children felt comfortable around him and wouldn't interact with him. It turned out to be for the best. He was caught trying to solicit a thirteen-year-old girl from California on the internet. What he got instead was a cybercop. He was arrested and his computer seized.

After Sparks and Brooks, no one was sure if they wanted to make another attempt to hire a youth pastor. When Jeff came and heard the accounts of the two before him, he asked the church for a two-month trial with no salary. Two years and hundreds of prayers later, and he's still here and everyone is happy.

"Anyway," Jeff said. "I thought I'd find you guys here. I just wanted to remind you all that we're having our VBS blowout tonight. I was wondering if you would stay late and help clean up after all the fun and games? There's also supposed to be pizza and refreshments afterwards."

"Pizza?" Plate said. "I'm in."

Everyone at the table laughed.

Everyone agreed.

"Cool! Thanks, I'll see you later. Bye."

Jeff turned to leave, and he almost bumped into Julie, again.

"We've gotta stop meeting like this," Jeff said.

Julie laughed and watched Jeff leave.

She turned and saw that they were looking at her.

"What? He's an attractive guy," Julie said, her cheeks getting red.

"We didn't say anything," Sarah said.

"Do you like him?" Ashley asked.

Julie looked around nervously. "Don't tell him, please."

"Julie, it's not our place to do so," Jess said. "You tell him when you're ready."

Julie placed the check on the table.

"Thanks," she said, relieved, and walked away.

Everyone at the table looked at each other, speechless.

Tim was the first to speak. "What was that all about?"

"I don't know," John said. "She's not married, no kids. Why's she so worried?"

"Men!" Jess, Sarah, and Ashley said in unison.

John laughed. "What?"

"She's shy," Jess said.

"Most likely, she doesn't want to get hurt," Ashley added.

"Oh," said Tim.

After a while of silence, John was the first to speak.

"Let's go to the church and see if Jeff needs our help with anything before VBS starts."

"Sounds good," Plate said. "Let's go."

They paid for their meal, left a tip and headed for the church.

As Liz was going through this week's paperwork, she heard a knock at the door.

Looking up, she saw Jack.

"Jack!" she said, standing. "Happy belated birthday!"

"Thanks, Liz."

"How was the trip? How's everyone?" She asked.

Jack smiled, walked up to her and gave her a kiss on the cheek. Liz was used to the familiarity of it all. Having worked with Jack these past few years, she's thought of him as a second father.

Liz and Jack sat down.

"So, how is everyone?" she asked again.

"Ah, great, great. Charlie and Samantha are adjusting to being grandparents, Jay and Heather are adjusting to being parents."

"And you're adjusting to being a great grandparent, right?"

Jack laughed. "That about sums it up, yeah."

Liz smiled. "What about you? You get some rest while you were down there?"

"Some," he said. "Being in the military all those years still has me getting up before everyone else."

"Some things never change."

"No, I guess not."

On the days Liz would get to work early, Jack would already be up and preparing for the day.

"Don't you ever sleep?" she would ask.

"Maybe," he'd say with a twinkle in his eye.

"Anyway," he said. "About change."

"What about it?"

"Well, Charlie's been asking me to retire and come down and stay close to the family."

"And? You said he's been asking you for some time now."

"He has."

"So?"

"So, I've been thinking about doing just that. I want to be close to my new great grandson. I want to watch him grow up for as long as I can."

"So, what's stopping you?"

Jack took a look around the office.

"This place. My grandfather built this place. My father helped run this place, then I took it over after my granddad died. He and my mom worked together to keep it going. Then they had me. When I was old enough, I helped out and went to school at the same time. Ella, too. Then, Pearl Harbor was attacked. I was so mad, Liz, I wanted to sign up right then in there! But I waited. I married Ella straight out of high school, then I went on to the military. We were both eighteen. By the time I was ready to be deployed, the war had ended."

"When I was twenty-one, we had Charlie. Ella was still helping run the restaurant with Mom and Dad."

"When he was sixteen, Charlie helped run things after my father died. I'd been in the service for nineteen years."

"I retired after twenty years in the service. Mom died, Charlie went to college, and me and Ella still continued to run the restaurant. Other than the military, this is all I ever did. It's all I've ever known. With Ella gone now, I think it might be good to move on, if it's the Good Lord's will."

Liz listened, then replied, "I think it would be a great idea. I mean, Jack, you just turned eighty-one. With the shape you are in, you could watch your great grandson grow up and become an adult. Do it!"

"One hundred years old!" Jack laughed. "You think so?"

"Be straight with me, Jack. There's something you're not telling me."

"I want you to have this place."

Liz couldn't believe what she had just heard.

"Excuse me?" she asked.

"Listen, Liz. There is no one outside my own family that I trust more than you. If I decide to retire, I want you to have this place."

Liz just stared blankly at Jack.

"Liz?"

"Me?"

"You have been like a daughter to me in these few short years. Jess, like a granddaughter. I don't want to give this place to some stranger who might do "who knows what" to what my grandfather built. I just want you to think about it, tell me later. I'm still thinking about all this myself."

"I'll think about it," Liz said.

Jack stood.

"That's all I ask. Now if you'll excuse me, I want to get home and unpack. I came here first to talk to you."

Liz stood up and gave him a hug.

Jack laughed. "I'll see you tomorrow."

"See you tomorrow."

As Jack left, Liz sat there thinking about what had just been said.

"Oh, Lord," Liz prayed. "What do you have planned?"

"Mom," Trisha said, gently nudging her mother.

"Mom."

No response.

"Mom! Earth to Annie! Wake up!" she said, shaking the bed.

"Huh? What's wrong? What is it?" Trisha's mom, Annie asked, panicked.

"It's time to wake up. You've got an hour before you go to work."

Annie sighed. "Thanks, honey. I've really got to get an alarm clock.

These shifts are gonna kill me. I might as well put up a cot in the back room."

"That might be a good idea. You'd at least get more sleep."

"Not funny, Little Miss," Annie said, stifling a yawn.

"It wasn't meant to be," Trisha said. "You said it yourself. These shifts are gonna kill you, if you don't get enough sleep."

Annie climbed out of her bed and walked down the small hall of their two-bedroom trailer and into the bathroom.

"Well, thankfully, when I get off at six tomorrow, I can sleep until Monday."

"That's if you're not told to stay another few hours."

"There is that," Annie said, washing her face. "Hopefully, I can still make it home for twelve hours of sleep."

Trisha decided to change the subject.

"Mom, do you think Kim and I could go to a sleep over tonight?"

Annie started the shower and asked, "Whose house?"

"Tammy's sister, Barb's house."

Annie thought for a moment. "No boys, right?"

"Mom..." Trisha said, rolling her eyes. "No boys. Just pizza, some movies, and some girl talk."

"I'm sure," Annie said smiling. "Girl talk about boys, no doubt, daring one another to call them and hang up."

Trisha looked at her mom. "Gee, Mom, you are getting old," she said playfully. "Calling boys and hanging up? Haven't you heard yet of text messaging?"

Trisha closed the door just as her mom threw a towel at her.

Annie laughed.

Through the door she said, "Fine. No boys, no problem, and don't bug the boys too much with your text messaging, okay?"

"Okay, Mom."

Trisha walked into the living room, sat down, and watched Kim play her video game.

"I told Mom we were going over to Tammy's sisters for the night," Trisha said.

Kim paused the game. "Why did you do that?"

"Because we will be going over there, it's on the way to the cemetery."

Kim just looked at her.

"Besides, Mom will be far too busy to even call and check up on us, not that she would, mind you. She hasn't yet."

"Whatever," Kim said, resuming her game.

A few minutes later, Annie walked into the living room.

"Alright. Time for me to go. Kim, be good and mind your sister. Have fun tonight."

"Okay, I will. Thanks, mom," Kim said.

Annie looked at her watch.

"Okay. I love you both. See you some time tomorrow."

"Love you, too, mom. Drive safely," Trisha said.

"Bye, Mom. Love you," Kim said.

After Trisha watched her mom leave, she looked at Kim.

"We'll leave in one hour," she said, leaving the living room.

"Fine. Whatever," Kim replied.

Trisha turned around and said, "Hey, if you don't want to come with me, you don't have to."

Kim paused her game once more.

"I want to come."

"Good," Trisha said, as she left the room.

"Home, sweet home," Jack said, unlocking the back door of his house. Jack tossed his keys onto the kitchen table and placed his suitcase on the empty chair.

"Now, what?" Jack said to himself.

He looked around and noticed his answering machine blinking.

"Probably a bunch of telemarketers trying to sell me something," he sighed, grabbing a glass out of the cupboard. "Let's see..." he said, opening the refrigerator door. "...Orange juice...apple...fruit punch...milk."

Jack stopped.

"Milk? Thought I drank it all before I left. It's gotta be bad by now."

Jack reached for the milk and checked the date.

"Sure enough," he said, checking the calendar on the wall. "Just a few days ago."

He went to the sink, turned on the water and dumped what was left of the milk down the drain.

"Orange juice it is," he said, pulling it out of the fridge.

Jack poured himself a glass and put the container back in the fridge. He then walked over to his answering machine and played the messages.

"You have four new messages and zero old messages," the answering machine said in an automated female voice. Jack rolled his eyes.

"I wish these things would just give me the messages without all this nonsense in between."

Finally, it got to the messages.

"Hello, Mr. Pippirelli," a nice friendly voice said.

"My name is Roxy and I work for a company called Unlimited Vacations..."

"I was right," Jack said, taking a sip of his juice. "Telemarketer."

"...and we are offering you the chance of a lifetime. How would you like a trip to Hawaii for a week? All expenses paid. All you would have to do is..."

"Ah, the catch," Jack said.

"...attend one lecture at the hotel you would be staying at. Not just any lecture, mind you. And not just any speaker. No, it will be Nicholas Kramer, the world's most renown leader in the supernatural. He will be speaking about the power of the mind, out-of-body experiences, hypnotism, and much, much more..."

"Message deleted," the automated voice said.

Jack shivered.

"Hypnotism, mind control..." he mumbled.

"New Age baloney and Demonic influences."

Jack listened to the next message.

"Hello, my name is Mr. Reed from Greater Communications, and I would like to know if your current Cable, Internet, and phone service provider is as cheap as we are."

"Message deleted."

Jack laughed.

"I'm already with you guys. Check your records."

The next message played.

"Oh," a voice said.

"I'm sorry. I think I have the wrong number. Sorry, God bless. Bye."

Jack smiled.

"So far the only decent thing left on my machine."

The last message played.

"Hello! How would you like to win a big-screen TV?"

"Message deleted."

"No, thanks, Bud," Jack said, downing the last of his orange juice.

"I'm happy with the one I already have."

Jack washed his glass, dried it, and put it back in the cupboard. He walked into the living room and sat down on his couch. He looked at the picture on top of the television set and smiled. It was a picture of him, Ella, Charles, Samantha, and Jay. It was taken a year before Ella's death.

"You'd be proud, honey," Jack said to the image of Ella.

"Jay married Heather and now they have a beautiful son. They named him Joseph. He's got your smile."

Jack looked around the room, then back at the picture.

"Charlie wants me to move and live closer to him."

Jack thought back to the conversation with Charlie.

"Dad? Why don't you stay?" Charles asked.

"Move here. You can live with me and Samantha."

"I still have my restaurant, Charlie. You know that."

"I know, Dad. I know. It's just...you don't need to work anymore. You worked your whole life. All I'm asking for is for me to take care of you."

"I can take care of myself," Jack said, smiling.

"Dad, what I mean is...I know you can take care of yourself, you're still in good shape. Heck, you might be in better shape than I am.

What I'm saying is this: I want you here with us. I want you to watch your great-grandson grow up. I also know you don't want anything to happen to the restaurant. Why don't you let Liz have it? You're always singing her praises about how good of a manager she is. I've seen how well she worked when I came to visit. Dad, she's like the daughter you never had."

Jack looked at him.

Charlie laughed.

"Oh, come on, Dad. Don't give me that look. The way you talk about her is the same way you talk about me. There's pride in your voice. A love in your voice. You're proud of her, just as you are of me. I can hear it in your voice, see it in your eyes when you talk about her."

"Really?"

"Dad, I know you want to keep the restaurant in the family..."

"I never said I expected you or Jay to take it over..."

"Dad, listen. I know. You wanted me to be what I wanted to be. You always supported me in what I wanted. No, you never said you wanted me to run the restaurant. But I know you. You want it to stay in the family. If you don't want to give the whole thing to Liz, make her part owner. Give her most of it. She's like family. It'll stay in the family."

"I'll pray about it, son."

"I just hope God will lead you here. I love you, Dad. I just want to spend more time with you."

"I know you do, son," Jack said, pulling Charlie in for a hug.

"I know you do."

Jack looked back at the family picture.

He then bowed his head.

"Lord," Jack prayed. "What is Your will?"

CHAPTER THREE

In the local cemetery, Mr. Stone stood, waiting for all The Faithful to arrive. Stone wore all black, blending into the shadow of the trees with the setting sun.

"Everyone's almost here," Trisha said.

When Trisha arrived with Kim, they found the twins talking with Stone.

"Are you the one?" she had asked.

"I am," Stone had replied.

Trisha nodded, then said, "Aaron and Lloyd, find yourselves a place to listen."

The boys did so without a word.

"I'll be looking at headstones while it's still light," Kim said.

"Okay, but when it starts, come stand by me," Trisha said.

Kim nodded and left.

"Cute kid," Stone said. "Is she your sister?"

"Yeah, she wants to hang around with me, so I let her. She doesn't understand what I like, and I think it scares her."

"After tonight," Stone said, "she'll understand a whole lot more, even if she doesn't want to."

The way he said that gave Trisha the creeps. *Should I send her home?* she thought.

Before she could decide, Stone said, "Listen up!" And waited just long enough to get everyone's attention. Kim came and stood by Trisha just as Stone was about to speak again. As everyone gathered around, Stone turned to Trisha and said, "Go into my briefcase. Inside, there are crystals with strings tied to them. Give everyone one."

Trisha did as she was told while Stone addressed everyone.

"First off, let me introduce myself to everyone. My name is Mr. Stone. I come on behalf of our master, Lucifer. Tonight, I am taking you to a place he has designated for his special purpose. It is a place of dreams, or nightmares, depending on what your personal outlook is. Other than the sixteen of you that are already here, we will be taking someone else who has been invited, she just doesn't know it yet. Her name is Jessica White. Our master has plans for her. Let's go welcome her to the party, shall we?"

As Stone finished, Kim became scared.

This sounds like a kidnapping! she thought.

What do I do?

As Kim was thinking, she heard Trisha talking to Mr. Stone.

"Mr. Stone," Trisha said. "There isn't one for Kim."

"Those were for The Faithful. As I understand it, she's not really part of it, is she?"

"No, I guess not," she said.

"Don't worry. She's still coming along, but she looks a little scared. Do you mind if I talk to her? I want to put her at ease."

She nodded.

Kim looked around. *Everyone looks fine with this! How can that be?*

"Kim?" Stone said.

"Huh?" she said, uncertain.

"You look frightened. Will you be alright?"

"I...I'm not sure," she answered, starting to feel sick.

"You know what I do when I'm scared? I say a little chant. You wanna try?"

Not knowing what to do, Kim nodded.

"That's a good girl, repeat after me." He began a soft chant.

Kim repeated the chant.

And her world went dark.

***

Michael, the archangel, sat on a bench across the street from the church recalling the last time Satan came and made his request.

"Satan!" God had said. "Where have you come from now?"

"From walking about the Earth," Satan replied.

"Somewhere in Midwest America; a small town called Forsaken & Forgotten. You remember it, don't you?"

"Why have you come here?" The Lord asked, ignoring the question.

"To seek Your permission to construct a world of my choosing to test the faith of one of Your followers."

"Who have you chosen?"

"A 16-year-old girl named Jessica White. Her parents are divorced, and she hasn't seen her father in years."

"How do you want to construct this world of yours?"

"By using the human's imaginations: Mythology, Movies, Books, Fairytales, Music, and all sorts of entertainment. I would be using life as well. With Your permission, I would also like to use a local cult for this, along with my angels, of course."

"You may. I will choose from My own to help this young lady."

"Ooh! You want to make this a game? Like saving the damsel in distress? I like it. It gives it more of a challenge, I think."

"Go! Construct your world."

"Thank you. I will be back."

When Satan had left, God called upon Michael.

"Yes, my Lord?" he had said.

"I have appointed you to help the humans I will choose for this."

"Yes, my Lord. Anything else?"

"Yes, I want you to choose as many angels as you think you will need to defeat Satan and his hordes of demons. It doesn't matter how many. They, as well as you will help guide My precious children through what Satan is planning."

"Yes, my Lord. I know just who to pick for this."

That had been just six months ago, according to the human calendar. Jessica would be 17 now. Michael continued to sit on the bench and wait. A bus pulled up and stopped. The bus door opened, and an elderly couple stepped out, nodding politely to Michael, smiling.

Michael nodded and returned the smile.

"Beautiful night, isn't it?" The elderly woman said, holding her husband's arm.

"Yes, it is," Michael said, as the couple walked away.

He then added, "God bless."

The woman turned and smiled.

"He has, richly," she replied as they walked away.

"Do you need a ride, Mister?" The bus driver asked, keeping the door open.

Michael looked at the bus driver, an older man in his mid-sixties.

"No, thank you, sir," Michael said.

"The name's Harold, Mister..."

"Michael. My name's Michael."

"I love that name," Harold said. "Every time I hear it, I think of the Archangel."

Michael smiled.

"Anyway, you sure you don't need a ride? No charge. I've been driving this baby all over town on a volunteer basis since I retired."

"Again," Michael said, "No, thanks. I'm just waiting."

Harold nodded. "Well, have a nice night. God bless," he said as he closed the bus door.

"You, too," Michael said as the door closed.

Harold gave a wave and pulled away.

"Almost time," Michael said as he watched the bus go.

Stone and The Faithful walked toward the church.

Stone looked across the street and noticed a man sitting on a nearby bench.

He snarled and said, "Looks like the players are in motion."

"What?" Trisha asked.

"Nothing," Stone said sharply. "I'm just thinking out loud."

Trisha nodded then looked at the rest of The Faithful. Her gaze fell on her sister, Kim. Ever since Stone took Kim aside, she seemed different. She was calm, no longer nervous.

Why does that have me so concerned? she thought.

You wanted her to relax and feel more at ease about this, didn't you?

Of course, I did.

Then what is the problem?

She didn't know. All she knew was her sister was acting differently.

"Alright," Stone said, "we wait here until she comes out. If she is with anyone, do not harm them too much. Is that understood?"

Everyone nodded in agreement.

"Good. Now we wait."

As they were waiting, Stone looked again across the street at Michael and glared. He thought about what one of his agents had said about how Ronald Stevens had moved here.

"Well, more for my amusement, I see," he had said. "I wonder if he'll even remember me?"

All he had to do was be patient. He could do that.

"Soon, very soon, my old friend..."

"He shoots! He scores!" Plate said, throwing a piece of paper in the trash can.

"Three points! And the crowd goes wild!" He said, imitating a cheering crowd

Jeff laughed. "Alright, Shaq, you can make a game of it, so long as we get this cleaned up by tonight."

"No problem," Plate said. "We're almost done anyways."

"Speak for yourself," Tim said. "I can't believe how many bags of garbage there are here tonight. What a mess."

"That's what happens after a week, and almost no clean up in between," Maggie Brooks said, coming in from another room.

"Thank our parents for that one," Ashley said.

"Taking a two-week honeymoon just as VBS is about to start."

"Does that mean you and I should have been cleaning up, Ashley?" Tim said.

"You, maybe, but not me," Ashley replied.

"Aw, come on, now," Tim teased.

"My mom's your mom now, Sis. We're family, and family helps out."

"Oh, give it a rest, Tim," Ashley said, trying hard not to laugh. "We've been like siblings even before our parents got hitched, anyway."

"Just makes it official now, Sis."

Ashley rolled her eyes. "Whatever, little bro."

"Only by a couple of months," Tim said.

"More like six," Ashley teased.

Tim and Ashley laughed and went back to work.

"Anyway," Maggie said, getting back on topic.

"We had more people here tonight. I think this was our best year yet!"

"That's just what I wanted to hear," Jeff said.

"By the way, Maggie, how are your classes going? It's been a busy week; I keep forgetting to ask."

"Crazy! By this time next year, you can call me Dr. Maggie."

Maggie had started going back to school to get her psychology degree shortly after she started counseling battered women like herself.

"I wanna be able to be an official counselor," she had told Pastor Stevens. "Someone everyone can take seriously."

"We take you seriously here," he had said.

"I know; I just want people to know that I know what I'm talking about."

Pastor Stevens smiled. "I think that would be a great idea."

"You will still have your office with the church, right?" Ashley asked.

"Don't worry. As long as the Lord wants me here, I'm staying."

"That's what I like to hear," Pastor Stevens said, walking into the room from the hallway.

"What's that?" Maggie asked.

"Keeping the Lord's will center in your life." Maggie smiled.

"So, Pastor Stevens," Jeff said, "what'd you think of VBS this week?"

"I think it was a good idea we were able to buy this place when we did. Look at this place! This is what the rest of the church would look like!" he said with a laugh.

The church had bought the large, empty lot next to the church just after VBS last year. They started construction right away and had it built in less than six months. They also built an edition from the church to the newly constructed building and put in a few offices, one of which was for Maggie, and designated the rest as a Rec center for the local kids, with different rooms of entertainment. They were all gathered in the main room.

"Honestly," Pastor Stevens said, "I think it went great. Do you know how many kids were saved this week?"

"I think maybe 7," Jeff said.

Pastor Stevens nodded and said, "That's great."

"Speaking of kids," Maggie said, "does any of you know who Bobby's parents are?"

"Bobby Baker?" Jeff asked. "No, I don't think so."

Jeff looked at Pastor Stevens, who just shook his head.

"I know who you're talking about, but no. Why?"

"I just wanted to call them and say what a special boy he is."

"Bobby?" Sarah asked, carrying a bag of trash.

"You're right, Maggie. He and John were talking about the Ten Commandments, and he recited from memory the whole thing, from four different versions of the Bible!"

"Which ones?" Jeff asked.

"Umm...King James, NIV, NLT, and ASV, I think."

Jeff whistled. "I can only memorize from one version of the Bible," he said with a laugh.

"It's not that hard if you practice."

Everyone turned to see who had said that. Standing in the doorway, stood Bobby.

"Oh, hi, Bobby," Maggie said.

"Hi, I left my Bible. I forgot it when I saw my dog, Lex, at the window just before the pizza party. I had to take him home."

"Well, if there's still some pizza left, you're welcome to it," Pastor Stevens told him.

"Yeah! I don't think Plate ate it all just yet," Sarah added.

Bobby smiled. "Thanks, do you need any more help cleaning up?"

"It's getting awfully dark," Jeff said. "What time do you need to be home?"

"My dad said it would be okay if I was here. I just have to call to let him know when I'm ready to be picked up."

"Okay," Jeff said. "We'd be happy if you helped."

Bobby smiled.

"Bobby," Sarah said. "You could start by eating up some of the leftover pizza and after you're finished, you can bring the garbage bags close to the side door."

"Okay, I can do that. No problem!" Bobby said.

After Bobby left, Maggie, Jeff, and Pastor Stevens exchanged looks.

"Do you think he was making it up? About his dad, I mean?" Maggie asked.

Pastor Stevens looked over to where Bobby was just starting to eat some pizza. "I don't know. But at least we know he's safe here."

Pastor Stevens said, looking bothered.

"Are you okay?" Jeff asked.

"Not really, no," he replied. "It's just this thing with Bobby. It just made me realize that we don't really know our neighbors. I mean that other than a few, almost everyone who comes to our church doesn't even live in this town. The kids come to church, but we never see their parents. Most of the kids for VBS have been member's nieces, nephews, or cousins. Something's gotta change."

"You're right," Maggie said. "But how do we do that?"

"I don't know. We need to pray about all this."

"Yeah," Jeff said.

After a minute of silence, Maggie was the first to speak.

"I think I'll help clean up with the others," she said, rushing off to work.

"Yeah, me too, I don't want to be here all night," Jeff replied.

"That makes three of us," Pastor Stevens said. "Morning Service is gonna come awfully early."

Someone stood at the front entrance and knocked.

"Deputy O'Neil," Pastor Stevens said. "What brings you by?"

Deputy Peter O'Neil, 28, had been coming to church since he was saved almost a year ago, whenever he could manage to get the day off.

"I saw the lights were on. I thought I'd check and see how everything was going."

"Oh, we just finished up VBS and the pizza party. Now, we're cleaning up. Well, everyone else is cleaning up. I'm about to go home."

Jeff came walking back by carrying a full trash bag.

"Hey, Peter," Jeff said, sitting down his burden.

"What's going on tonight for our local Deputy?"

"If you'll excuse me," Pastor Stevens said. "I gotta go. Good night."

"Good night, Pastor," Jeff and Peter said.

"Anyway," Jeff said as Pastor Stevens left, "What's happening?"

"Well, I just came from the cemetery. Mrs. Jenkins called in a complaint saying that there were a bunch of teens sneaking in just after sunset.

"She thought it might have been The Faithful. We're always getting calls about teen vandalism, just minor stuff. It's usually them. Anyway, I went and checked it out.

"I didn't see much of anything, though."

Jeff was well aware of the gang. He had seen the name "The Faithful" sprayed on a few old houses outside of town. He suspected that it was some kids in the next town, given the vicinity of the tagging.

"I really wish I could reach those kids, or even see them, for that matter."

"Yeah," Peter said. "Have you seen the new stuff they're doing?"

"No," Jeff said, "Not this week. Why?"

"Well, the tagging has gotten more disturbing."

"Disturbing, really?" Jeff asked. "How disturbing?"

"They have, using spray paint, painted cloaked figures in a circle. In the circle, there's a figure that looks like the devil."

"I hope it's just scare tactics," Jeff said with a shudder.

"Yeah," Peter said, looking uncomfortable.

"Hey, is, um, Maggie here, by any chance?" He asked, trying to change the subject.

"I might be, but you gotta turn around," Maggie said with a laugh.

"Oh, hey," Peter said.

"I'll let you two talk," Jeff said as he lifted his trash bag and carried it off.

"Thanks," Peter said.

Maggie and Peter had gone out a few times. Lately, it's been hard because of her schooling, his shifts at the Sheriff's office, and more recently, planning VBS. At first, Maggie wasn't sure about dating. After T.J. and all.

"I'm not sure what to do," she had told Pastor Stevens when Peter had asked her out. "I'll think about it," she had told him.

"Maggie," Pastor Stevens had said. "Pray about it. See where the Lord leads you. Peter is a nice young man. I know you haven't gone out with anyone since..."

"T.J. killed himself," Maggie finished.

"Yes, since then. Pray about it, Maggie. Please."

And she did. Not only did she have peace about dating Peter, but she realized that he actually made her feel really alive for the first time since T.J.

"So," Maggie said, "what's up?"

"Not a whole lot," Peter said. "I've been busy. How's school?"

"It's been crazy busy. Next week I graduate...then maybe we could go out to celebrate?"

Peter smiled. "I'd like that. When's the big day?"

"Next Friday."

"I'll see if I can get the day off then, or trade with someone."

Maggie smiled. "That sounds great."

"Maggie," Jeff called. "Could you go get the box I put in your office for safekeeping, please?"

"Yeah, sure, Jeff." She looked at Peter and said, "Work here never ends."

While Maggie went to get the box, Peter laughed and said, "Don't I know it."

"Okay, everybody," Jeff said. "Break time! Gather 'round"

Everybody stopped what they were doing to see what Jeff wanted.

"As soon as Maggie gets back, we have something for you. For all of the hard work, you've done this past week. But first, I want to thank each of you for helping. Maggie, me, and the other teachers couldn't have done it without the help of the five of you."

"We loved every minute of it," Ashley said.

"I know. And I thank you. As soon as Maggie... ah, here she comes."

Maggie came back carrying a medium-sized box.

"You need some help with that, Maggie?" Peter asked.

"No, I got it. Thanks, though," Maggie replied

"Just sit it on the table, please," Jeff said.

Maggie did as instructed. The box landed with a loud thud.

"Thanks, Maggie."

Jeff opened the box.

"Guys, we had these custom made for you. It's like a Blueberry, Blackberry, or whatever they are called. Anyway, it has different versions of the Bible, concordances, study helps, daily devotions, and a few other really cool things, and it can fit in your pocket for convenience. Maggie's been tinkering around with one of them. Here, Jess."

Jeff tossed Jess a small box.

"Open it. Take a look."

"What do you call those things?" Plate asked.

"Well, the people wanted to call it the Godberry. I'd rather call it a Bible, but we'll see. Thankfully, the company that made these just let us have them. They said something about us being testers of a new device."

Jess opened the box and found instructions and a slim case. She flipped the case open and turned it on.

"Wow. It's small, but you can see the screen perfectly. Thanks."

Everyone said thank you after receiving one.

"Bobby?" Jeff said. "Would you like one too?"

"No, thanks, but thank you."

"You're welcome," Jeff said. "Okay, guys. What's left to do?"

"Just take the garbage out, and then we're done," Jess said, putting her Bible in her back pocket.

"Good, good. Do you think you guys can handle that part while Maggie and I start locking up and shutting off most of the lights?"

"Sure," John said, putting the small box back down on the table.

"I'll get the lights," Peter said.

The others also put their boxes on the table and got back to work.

"What a great week," Sarah said as they opened the side door to the ally. "I think this was our best VBS ever!"

"You're not the only one," Jess said. "I heard Pastor Stevens and Jeff saying the same thing."

A dog barked.

"Aw, man," Bobby said.

"What?" John asked.

"Lex. He got out again."

No sooner had he said that, Lex came running into the alley.

"Lex, how'd you get out again?"

"Cute dog," Jess said, as she put a trash bag in the dumpster.

"Thanks," Bobby said.

Suddenly, the alley light went out.

Lex growled.

"What is it, boy?" Bobby asked.

"Jessica White?" A voice asked.

Jess looked around to see who called her.

There, standing at the entrance to the alley from the street, stood a tall man in all black. Others, in black cloaks, stood next to him.

"That's him," Jess let out a stunned whisper.

"That's the guy from in front of Pips."

Tim, who was a couple of feet from Jess asked the guy, "What do you want?"

"We are having a party," the man said. "Jessica is our guest of honor."

"I don't like this," John said. "Bobby, take Lex and get Deputy O'Neil."

"But I..."

"Do it!" John and Plate both said in unison.

Bobby and Lex bolted for the door.

"She's not going anywhere with you," John said. "Tim, get her outta here."

"Come on, Jess," Tim said, touching her arm.

She wouldn't move. She was frozen with fear.

"His eyes..." she said.

"That is where you are wrong, my young friend," the man said to John.

"I'm not your friend, and you're not taking her."

The man removed his shades and said, "Now."

Without warning, the cloaked figures moved with lightning speed and pushed John, Tim, and Plate away from Jess, knocking them to the ground. Another figure grabbed a garbage can lid and threw it at Sarah and Ashley. Sarah grabbed Ashley and pulled her to the ground.

Ashley screamed as the disk whizzed by. They grabbed Jess and ran toward a door that suddenly appeared out of nowhere.

That wasn't there before! A stunned Tim thought as he tried getting up, shaking his head for clarity. The alley light went back on. The door opened, and everyone jumped in, taking Jess with them.

The door slammed shut.

"No!" Tim screamed as he got up and ran to the door.

He opened the door, but nothing was there. Nothing but the other side of the alley. Tim shut the door and leaned on the door frame, sliding down.

Oh, God, Tim prayed as he noticed a man walking from across the street to the alley. *What just happened?*

CHAPTER FOUR

"Lord," Pastor Stevens prayed as he got into his car, "Thank You for another great year for VBS." He smiled as he thought about Maggie and her coming graduation. "Thank you for bringing her healing and helping her grow..."

Pastor Stevens started his car and thought about the faithful night that changed her life...

Pastor Ronald Stevens had gone to the Brooks' house to ask T.J. about the theme for Vacation Bible School so he could put it in the monthly newsletter, only to find him drunk in the front yard, shouting profanities at anyone in earshot. Maggie, Brooks' wife could be heard crying somewhere in the house.

"Shut up, woman!" Brooks had said. "Before I come in there and shut you up real good!"

As Pastor Stevens got out of his car, one of the neighbors shouted to him, "He's been like this now for about two hours, Pastor. We've been hearing yelling and screaming inside, then he started out here. We finally called the police about twenty minutes ago."

Steven nodded. Walking slowly toward the Brooks' house, he said, "T.J., what's wrong? Why have you been drinking?"

That only got a volley of profanities thrown at him.

Pastor Stevens winced. He hadn't heard that many profanities since he got rid of his television set.

"T. J., can I help you? What's wrong?"

Brooks started mumbling.

"Maggie!" Pastor Stevens yelled into the house. "You okay in there?"

All he could hear was her crying.

"Be with that young lady in there, Father," he prayed.

He could hear the sirens getting close.

"The police are coming, I hear them," someone shouted.

That only got Brooks even more angry.

"Let them come," he said with a string of more profanities. "I'll teach 'em!"

"Teach them what, T.J.?" Pastor Stevens asked, trying to get his attention.

Brooks looked at Pastor Stevens and swore again.

Slowly, Pastor Stevens walked toward T.J. and said, "T.J., it's me, Ron, from church. Can't we talk? Tell me what the problem is. Maybe I can help!"

Brooks said something.

"What?" Pastor Stevens asked, getting closer. "I didn't hear you."

As the police sirens got louder, Brooks took a swing at Pastor Stevens. He avoided the punch and grabbed Brooks' arm and pushed him to the ground. Pastor Stevens kept Brooks' arm behind his back, pinning him down.

"Get off of me!" Brooks screamed.

"Not until the police arrive."

Brooks screamed again.

After what felt like forever, the police and EMS arrived, and they helped Pastor Stevens off of Brooks, who was still swearing, cuffed him, and put him in the squad car. While all that was going on, Pastor Stevens went inside the house to check on Maggie.

"Maggie!" Pastor Stevens called. "Where are you?"

"I..in the k..kitchen," she said through sobs.

When he got to the kitchen, he saw her on the floor, the China cabinet pinning her legs.

"Hey!" Pastor Stevens said through the open window.

"I need some help in here!"

Turning his attention back to Maggie, he asked, "Are you okay?"

She continued to cry.

"Oh, Maggie," he said. "Has he done this before?"

Maggie looked at the Pastor, only to reveal a black eye and busted lip.

"He didn't mean to," she sobbed. "H...he's tried to stop."

Pastor Stevens looked at her. "Maggie, how long has this been going on?"

"Two, maybe three years. He started when we lost the baby. He couldn't handle it."

He remembered when they first met in his office four weeks ago, they talked about family.

Maggie had had a miscarriage in her sixth month.

That was three and a half years ago.

"He doesn't mean to hurt me. He loves me...I love him."

Pastor Stevens' temper flared. He could never stand for a woman to make excuses for her husband or boyfriend when it came to mental or physical abuse. Before he could say anything that he might regret, the paramedics arrived to check her over. Maggie sustained a broken rib, a twisted ankle, and some bruising, with no permanent physical damage.

Later that night, Brooks assaulted an officer at the station. Brooks went to prison for assault and other counts of battery. Maggie went to counseling.

A couple of months after being sent to prison, he was found hanging in his cell with a note:

Maggie, I am so sorry for hurting you. I don't want to hurt anyone else. I cannot stand this pain. I love you. Goodbye.

-T.J.

Later, she started a program for battered and abused women at the church.

You are a good God, even in the darkness of despair. Thank you.

As Stevens continued to drive, he became bothered. Almost like he forgot something.

"I didn't take anything to the church with me, except my Bible," he thought out loud. His Bible lay on the passenger seat, but something still nagged at him in the back of his head. As he stopped at the red light, he tried to think about what he might have forgotten.

What am I missing? What is out of place?

A horn honked behind him. The light was green. He drove again while thinking.

Go back to the church.

Pastor Stevens jumped. He knew Whose voice it was. He had heard it many times in his life.

"Lord," he prayed while making a U-turn to head back to the church, "What is it?"

Nothing but silence. Taking a different approach, he quoted Samuel:

"Speak, Lord; for thy servant heareth."

You are needed. Go back to the church.

Stevens sighed. Something was going on at the church, and he needed to be there. As he drove, he prayed.

In the back office of Pippirelli's Pizza, Liz sat in her chair, finishing up the last of the day's paperwork.

"Another day, another dollar, and more paperwork to show for it," Liz said. "Well, that's the last of it."

She looked at her watch. "I finished earlier than I thought I would. How nice for a change."

As Liz walked out of the office, she saw Jack and Julie putting the chairs up on the tables.

"Is Toby and the girls gone?" Liz asked Julie.

"Yeah," Julie said, putting up a chair. "Cindy and Jane helped Toby clean the kitchen, then they left together."

"I told them they could go home after they helped him clean up," Jack said.

"I thought you went home," Liz said to Jack.

"And now I'm back," Jack said, smiling. "I didn't feel like staying home, and I didn't want to go out anywhere, so I came here."

"But here is anywhere," Liz teased.

"Ah! But here is home, too. Besides, I enjoy the company here."

"Maybe you should get a dog," Julie said.

Jack laughed. "I've never been an animal person. I mean, I love animals, but they don't seem to like me. Anyway, I prefer the company of lovely ladies."

"Even if they are old enough to be your daughter and granddaughter," Liz said with a laugh.

"Now, come on," Jack said laughing. "You know I wouldn't rob the cradle."

"I know, that's why we love you."

"Of course," Jack said, rubbing his chin, "there's always a first time for everything."

Julie gasped.

"Dirty old man," she said, grabbing a rag she was cleaning the tables with and throwing it at him.

The trio burst out laughing.

"Okay, okay," Jack said, regaining his composure.

"Honestly, I would never do that. There has only been one woman in my life, and that was my Ella. I knew her my whole life. I even think my mom said we used to take bubble baths together as babies."

"That really is your whole life, isn't it?" Julie said.

Jack nodded. "It's like I was telling Liz in the back earlier, I've only known this place, except where the military took me."

Everyone was quiet for a moment.

"Well," said Jack, "these chairs aren't going to put themselves up. Let's get back to work."

They worked in silence.

To be with someone your whole life, then suddenly have them pulled away from you without any warning, Liz thought. *That must have been really hard on him when that happened.*

Pray for Jessica, a voice whispered to Liz.

"Huh?" Liz said, startled.

"You okay, Liz?" Jack asked.

"Yeah, I'm fine. I thought I heard something," Liz said.

Jack nodded and went back to work.

"Lord," Liz silently prayed. "Is that You? What's going on?"

For where two or three are gathered together in My Name, there I am in the midst of them.

"What is it, Lord?" Liz asked.

Pray for Jessica.

Liz grabbed the closet chair and began to cry.

"Liz?" Jack spoke, "Liz are you alright?"

Jack and Julie both came to Liz's side.

"Liz," Jack said, "are you okay?"

"I don't know what's going on, but we need to pray for Jessica," Liz said. "Something's not right. She should still be at the church..."

"I'll tell you what," Jack said. "You and Julie stay here and pray, and I'll go over to the church and see what's going on, alright?"

Liz dabbed at her eyes with a tissue that Julie had handed her.

"Yes, please. Would you?"

"Sure thing."

As Jack walked to the exit and opened the front door, he looked back at Liz and Julie, who were already huddled in prayer.

"Lord," Jack prayed while he walked out the door. "I don't know what's going on, but protect Liz and Jess. They are two very special people who are a very important part of my family."

As Tim leaned against the door frame, a tall man walked up and grabbed it.

"Excuse me," Tim said standing, ready to fight.

"What are you doing?"

The man did not speak. Instead, he lifted the frame.

"Hey!" Tim said. "What are you doing with that?! Who are you?"

The man did not speak, making Tim angrier.

"Hey! I'm talking to you."

The man started walking to the entrance of the church Rec area.

Tim grabbed his arm and said, "Who are you?"

The man looked at Tim and finally spoke.

"I am taking the door inside. I suggest you check on your friends while I do so."

Tim suddenly remembered everyone else and looked around.

He saw Sarah and Ashley helping John and Plate to their feet. Tim ran to his friends and asked, "Are you guys okay?"

Everyone looked around checking for broken bones, cuts, or bruises. Everyone was fine.

"Hey," John said, pointing to the stranger, "who's that?"

"He wouldn't tell me," Tim replied.

At that time, Peter and Jeff came running out the side door.

They saw the kids dusting themselves off, then noticed the Stranger.

"Michael?!" Jeff said. "What are you doing here?"

Tim came running up. "Michael? Jeff, you know this guy?"

Before Jeff could reply, the Stranger named Michael said, "Finish with the trash."

"What? Who are you? What is happening?" Tim started to protest.

"Tim," Jeff said, "do what he says. I don't know what's going on, but I'm sure it will all be explained."

"But..."

Jeff put his hand on Tim's shoulder.

Tim looked at Jeff.

Jeff looked back. "Please."

"Okay," Tim said, still upset.

Peter looked confused. "Bobby just came in yelling something about a guy wearing sunglasses, and a bunch of people wearing black cloaks. What happened?"

"Peter," Jeff said, "would you help them with the trash? I need to talk with Michael."

"Okay," Peter said, still confused.

Michael picked the door frame back up, and he and Jeff started walking back into the church's Rec area.

"Michael, I haven't seen you since..."

As Jeff and Michael walked into the church, Peter looked at the kids and asked, "What happened? Where's Jess?"

"The door," Tim mumbled.

"What?" Peter asked.

"Let's get the trash taken out before anything else," John said.

"I want to know what happened, too, and who that Michael person is. Jeff seems to know him."

They worked in silence for the remainder of the time it took to deal with the rest of the trash. When they were done, they all walked back in and saw Jeff talking with Michael, the door between them.

"Where's Bobby?" Sarah asked.

"Over here," came the voice of Maggie.

They turned and saw Maggie and Bobby sitting in the corner, petting Lex.

"You okay, Bobby?" John asked.

"Sure," Bobby said.

Tim walked up to Michael and demanded, "Okay, who are you? What are you doing here? And most importantly, what the heck happened to Jessica?!"

"Whoa," Plate said. "Easy there, Cue Ball. Relax a bit."

Before Tim knew it, he was lunging at Plate.

John held him back.

"Now's not the time for your stupid nicknames, *Paul*! I want to know what happened to Jess and I want to know now!"

"Tim, calm down," Ashley said. "Attacking Plate isn't going to help anything right now."

"Sorry, Tim," Plate said, putting his hand on his shoulder.

Tim sank to the floor and started to cry.

"I was right by her," he said through sobs. "They hit me hard. I saw them take her. They carried her through that door."

Tim pointed to the door and said, "And then they vanished."

"No one is blaming you for any of this, Tim," John said.

After a few seconds, Tim composed himself, looked at Michael, and asked, "If you know what's going on, would you please tell us?"

"I will tell you what I know, but first, you tell us what happened a few moments ago."

Tim sighed.

"Okay, we were taking out the trash when Bobby's dog, Lex, came running up. After a few seconds, he started growling and this guy...me and Jess saw him earlier outside of Pips. Anyway, this guy calls out her name and says that she has been invited to something. Something about her being the guest of honor. He had a bunch of other people in black cloaks with him."

John spoke up. "I didn't like what was being said, so I told Bobby to get out of there and go inside to get Deputy O'Neil and Jeff. The next thing I know, I'm being pushed off my feet landing in a pile of garbage, and Plate landing on me."

"Yeah," Plate said. "Sorry."

"Anyway," Tim continued. "I was trying to get Jess inside, but she seemed to be frozen with fear. She wouldn't move. She said that he had soulless blue eyes. I was knocked down, and they grabbed her. The door appeared out of nowhere, and they carried her through it. Once I regained my bearings, I ran to the door, opened it, and found nothing except the other side of the alley. That's where you came in."

Tim directed the last statement to Michael.

Michael nodded.

"Now I will tell you all I know. First, I am Michael, the Archangel of God. Second, I am here to help you bring Jessica back home safely. And third, Jessica has been taken by Satan's forces."

"Whoa, whoa, whoa," Plate said. "Wait a minute, here! Let me get this straight. You're Michael? *The Michael?* You mean the one from the Bible?"

"One and the same," Michael replied.

"Okay...Now could you explain the rest of what you just said?"

"Just a few human months ago, Satan came before the Throne of the Almighty and said he wanted to destroy Jessica's soul by having her renounce Christ. He was granted permission to design a world of his choosing to accomplish that end, which is where the door comes in. It is the way into that world."

"Is she...will she be okay?" Tim asked, looking at the door.

"He was given instructions not to hurt her physically."

"That leaves psychology, emotionally and spiritually," Maggie said. "That's all very important to a person."

"Yes," Michael said.

"How are we going to help her?" John asked.

Michael looked around and then said, "You each have your own strengths and skills. Some you already know; others will be revealed to you in time."

"What do you mean 'revealed to you in time?' Are you talking supernatural/spiritual?" Plate asked.

"All will be revealed in time," Michael answered.

"Are you always this cryptic?" Maggie asked.

"Yes," Jeff replied.

Everyone looked at Jeff.

"Jeff, how is it you know Michael, anyway?" John asked.

"Well..." Jeff started.

"That is a story for another day," Michael said.

"Let me guess," Plate said. "'All will be revealed in time,' right?"

Michael gave him a look.

Plate cleared his throat. "Sorry," he muttered.

"Um... shouldn't I be reporting this?" Peter asked.

"I mean, this is a kidnapping, and I am an officer of the law."

"No," Michael said. "There will not be a need for that."

"What are we to do first, then?" Tim asked. "I mean, Jess has been kidnapped, and we're just sitting here."

"First," Michael said, "you need to start praying. Satan's design for his world involves all sorts of things. He will use anything to stop you from your goal. You will need all your armor for this battle."

"The whole Armor of God, right?" Plate asked.

Michael smiled.

"Put on the whole armor of God, that ye may be able to stand against the wiles of the devil."

"For we wrestle not against flesh and blood, but against principalities,

against powers, against the rulers of the darkness of this world, against spiritual wickedness in high places."

"Wherefore take unto you the whole armor of God, that ye may be able to withstand in the evil day, and having done all, to stand."
"Stand therefore, having your loins girt about with truth, and having on the breastplate of righteousness; And your feet shod with the preparation of the gospel of peace."

"Above all, taking the shield of faith, wherewith ye shall be able to quench all the fiery darts of the wicked. And take the helmet of salvation, and the sword of the Spirit, which is the word of God."

"Okay, that's for the spiritual part of it," Tim said. "Do we also get real armor and weapons?"

"Do not underestimate the 'spiritual part' of it, young sir. Yes, you will be getting other weaponry, whatever you want, but God's Armor is just as equally important."

"No, correct that. It is more important."

"Um...Michael," John said. "Before you say anything else that we really need to hear, will you give me a couple of minutes with Tim?"

"Certainly," Michael replied.

John walked away and motioned Tim to follow.

Jeff cleared his throat and said, "I think while we wait for John and Tim, I think it would be best if we would pray together. Would you mind joining hands while I lead us in a word of prayer?"

As Pastor Stevens pulled up in the church parking lot, he saw Jack Pippirelli walking up to the church.

"Jack!" Pastor Stevens called. "How was your vacation?"

Jack stopped and turned around.

"Pastor, I'd love to talk about it, but right now I've gotta get inside the church to see how Jessica is."

"Jessica? What do you mean?"

"Well, Liz has a strong feeling that something is wrong with Jessica. She and Julie are back at the restaurant praying while I check up on things."

Pastor Stevens frowned. "Something's up. The Lord told me I was needed here. Come with me, everyone should be in the Rec area cleaning up after the VBS blowout."

Jack and Pastor Stevens walked around to the other side of the church and opened the door. When they walked in, they heard Jeff's voice in prayer. The two men stood silent so that they wouldn't be disturbing the prayer. As they waited, they noticed the tall man there and a door just to the side of where they were praying. Neither one could make out what was being said, though. And neither one wanted to get closer to disrupt them. So, they waited.

John opened Maggie's office door and waited for Tim to also enter. When he entered, John closed the door and smacked the back of Tim's head.

"Ow! What was that for?" Tim asked as he turned around, rubbing the back of his head.

"You're acting like an idiot out there! Calm down."

"Jess has just been kidnapped, and you want me to calm down?"

"Yes, you're not doing anyone any good acting like this. You are giving Michael way too much attitude. You may not believe he is who he says he is, but I sure do. Jeff even knows him somehow, and I'd like to know how."

"I never said I didn't believe who he says he is. I just saw a bunch of strange things happen already like Jess being taken through some door to nowhere. Of course, I believe he is who he says he is."

"Then why are you giving him trouble?"

"What about Plate? He's giving Michael sarcasm."

"This isn't about Plate, it's about you. He's always like that, and you know it."

Tim looked down.

"Hey, look. We all love Jess and we're all concerned for her safety. I also know that your feelings for her are stronger than that of just friendship."

Tim looked up with tears in his eyes.

"How do you know? I haven't even told her, or anyone else for that matter."

"You don't need to say it. I see the way you look at her, the way you react when someone mentions her name. And I saw it when you were yelling at Michael."

Tim nodded.

"But listen, if you are going to be of any help in getting her back from where she is, you are going to have to calm down and get your act together. I would start by apologizing to Michael for talking to him the way you did."

"More like yelled at him, you mean," Tim said.

"Yeah, that's what I mean."

Tim hugged John.

"Thanks, I needed a good talking to. Do you think Jess knows I like her?"

"I don't know. She's not as easy to read as you are. I mean, c'mon, I hang out with you, one on one, all the time. When have Jess and I ever been alone?"

"Yeah," Tim said. "Good point."

"Are you ready to go back out there?" John asked.

Tim nodded. "Yeah, I think I am."

John opened the door and walked out of the office.

As they walked back to the group, they could hear Jeff closing in prayer.

"... in Your Son's Holy name, we pray. Amen."

As Jeff finished, Jack and Pastor Stevens walked up.

"Jeff," Pastor Stevens said. "There's something going on, what is it?"

"Where's Jessica?" Jack added.

"She has been taken," Michael said.

Jack and Pastor Stevens both looked at Michael.

"I don't believe we've met," Pastor Stevens said. "I'm Ronald Stevens, the Pastor here. And you are?"

"Michael, Archangel of God."

Pastor Stevens looked at Jeff.

"It's true. Some weird things happened shortly after you left."

"Please, tell me," Pastor Stevens said.

"In short," Michael explained, "Satan has had Jessica kidnapped and taken to his world through the door over there," Michael said, pointing to the door.

"What?" Pastor Stevens and Jack asked together, apparently trying to absorb all of what they were hearing.

"A man in all black and a bunch of people in black cloaks grabbed Jess and took her through the door," John said.

"Oh, man," Jack said. "Liz was right. Something is wrong. What on Earth am I going to tell her?"

"Bring her here," Michael said. "Tell her the truth and let her know that she is needed here."

Without a second thought, Jack bolted out as fast as possible to get Liz.

"I didn't know he could move that fast," Jeff muttered.

"He really loves the Whites," Michael said.

"Michael," Pastor Stevens said, "would you please tell me what's going on?"

"Satan wants to destroy Jessica's soul. He will use any means necessary to achieve his goal. He is also using a local cult to achieve his plans, The Faithful."

At the mention of The Faithful, Jeff paled as he looked at Peter.

"Were they at the cemetery tonight?" Peter asked.

"Yes," Michael said. "They were getting their instructions from one of Satan's agents. He calls himself Mr. Stone."

Color drained from Pastor Stevens' face.

"S-Stone? Does he still inhabit the same body as before?"

Michael looked at Pastor Stevens and said, "I know of your encounter with him."

"Yes, he has the same body."

"You know that maniac?" Tim asked.

"I-it was a long time ago." He looked back at Michael and said, "Without Jay's help, I may not be here. Where is he now?"

"He's on assignment. He is somewhere in Asia. That's all I can tell you."

Pastor Stevens nodded.

"Who's Jay?" Plate asked.

"He's an angel who helped me with this Mr. Stone. It was some time ago."

"Um...guys?" Tim said. "I don't want to be rude."

He looked over at Michael and said, "By the way, I'm sorry about my outburst, I'm just worried."

"I understand," Michael replied.

"Anyway," Tim said trying to make his point, "Michael here hasn't finished telling us what we need to do to go get Jess."

"I will tell you all as soon as Jack brings Jessica's mother over," Michael said.

"In the meantime, I suggest that you all take some time to pray. Pray for the strength you will need for this journey. Pray for guidance. Pray for wisdom and," Michael said, looking at Tim, "pray you will have patience."

"Yeah, I guess I'm lacking there, aren't I?" Tim said.

Plate put his arm around Tim and said, "I think we all lack in that area, at times, buddy."

Everyone walked away and found a spot to pray. They prayed for themselves and each other and what they were about to face. They prayed for Jessica. But most of all, they prayed for her very soul.

CHAPTER FIVE

Jess awoke with a feeling of dread. The last thing she remembered was being attacked in the ally and being pushed through a door. Slowly, she opened her eyes and took in her surroundings. She was lying down, in a well-lit room. She could see the ceiling, grey in color. She looked to see what she was lying on. A small cot, grey as well. She sat up and looked around. The room she was in was all grey, like a prison cell. A window on one wall and a mirror on the other nothing in between except the cot.

Jessica stood up and started to walk toward the window when she heard a voice say, "Ah, so you've awakened, have you?"

Jessica jumped. She recognized that voice. The man with the cold eyes.

"What do you want with me?" she cried.

The voice gave a soft, evil chuckle. She noticed a small speaker in the top corner of the mirror.

Must be a two-way, she thought.

"As I said, you are our guest of honor. The master has some special plans involving you."

"No, thanks," Jess said.

He chuckled again. "You really have no choice, Miss White."

"I'm afraid you have me at a disadvantage," Jess said, faking bravado.

"Who might you be?"

"Ah, yes. Pardon me for being so rude. You may call me Mr. Stone. Or Stone if you prefer."

Jess looked around again, looking for a way out of the room.

"If you are looking for a way out, I suggest you don't. Oh, you would be able to fit through the window, but it's a long way down, I can assure you."

Jessica walked to the window, looked out, and gasped. The sky and the ground both had a reddish color to it. Even the water seemed red.

In the air were strange flying creatures, some looking like they came off the pages of books on mythology and dinosaurs. Others were similar to creatures she had seen in the movies. The same went for the creatures on land and water.

"Where am I?"

"A place of imagination," he said.

Not my imagination, she thought. *Nightmare is more like it.*

Jess looked out the window. She would be able to fit through it, but she didn't want to try it.

Not yet.

"I'll let you get used to your new room. In the meantime, you can listen to some music."

Stone's evil chuckle could be heard just before the music started playing. If you could call it music, it was loud, and the lyrics were evil and vulgar, and it violated her very soul. Jessica felt a wave of nausea as she covered her ears and prayed, in hopes of drowning it out.

"Well," Stone said, looking at the two other occupants in the room, "that should keep her occupied for a while. Feel free to change things up while I'm gone."

"Yes, sir," Kim replied as Stone started to leave the room.

"Wait," Trisha said. "Where are you going?"

Stone turned around and with a smile replied, "Fishing."

Before Trisha could ask another question, Stone vanished.

"How did he do that?" she thought out loud.

"Carefully," Kim replied with a strange smile.

Trisha looked at her sister. *What's up with her? Just a few couple of hours ago she was uneasy about all this.*

She shook the thought away.

As long as she wasn't in the way and helping, why worry?

"So, what do you want to do?" Trisha asked.

"Do you want to stay here, controlling the room, or do you want to look around for a bit?"

"I think I'll stay here," Kim replied. "You go ahead."

"Okay, I'll be back in a few minutes. If you need me, use the intercom, okay?"

"Sure," Kim replied, focusing her attention back on Jess through the two-way mirror. As Trisha was leaving the room, she heard Kim say, "Now the real fun begins," with a laugh.

What have I gotten her into, she thought. *What have I gotten us into?*

As Jack reached the diner, he was thankful not to be out of breath. *Good thing I stayed in shape*, he thought. As he opened the door, he saw Julie and Liz, still together praying. He cleared his throat.

"Liz," he said.

Liz and Julie looked up.

"What is it? Is anything wrong? Is Jessica okay?"

Jack walked up to Liz and put a hand on her shoulder.

"I don't entirely know what's going on, but I need you to come with me without any questions. Do you think you can do that?"

Liz looked on the verge of tears.

"Liz? Can you do that for me?"

Liz nodded, unsure of anything.

"That's a good girl," Jack said.

He then said to Julie, "Here are my car keys. Will you go start it up, please?"

Julie reached for the keys and nodded. Jack looked back at Liz.

Oh, Lord, Jack prayed. *Be with her. Give us the strength to deal with this.*

"Liz, let's go to my car, okay?"

Liz nodded fighting tears. As Jack walked Liz to his car, he did the only thing he knew he could do: He prayed.

As the young man walked up the street, he saw a car pull into a church parking lot. The man stopped and watched as three people got out of the vehicle - one man and two women - and went into the building connected to the church. The man proceeded to walk past the church, searching for the fallen angels. He felt their presence drop in around the area just a short time ago.

"Where are you?" He said to himself. "You were here, now where did you go?"

He continued to walk past the church. He then stopped when he felt a familiar presence. Not that of the ones he was looking for, but... purer.

"Michael," the man whispered. "What would be so important that the Archangel himself would be here? Is the time so close that you are hunting down the fallen ones as well?"

The man shook his head.

"No, not you."

"But why are you here?"

The man walked up to the building and opened the door.

As Jack and Julie led Liz into the hall, Pastor Stevens and Peter came to meet her.

"Elizabeth," Pastor Stevens said.

"Pastor Stevens," Liz replied. "Where is Jessica?"

"She's not here," Jeff said, bringing her a chair.

"What do you mean, 'she's not here?'" Liz asked as she sat down. "Where is she?"

"Allow me to explain things," a man Liz had never seen before said.

"First: My name is Michael, the Archangel of God. Second: Your daughter has been taken by the forces of Satan."

Liz didn't know where to begin. "Michael--Archangel--Satan," she stammered, trying to let it all sink in. "What happened to my Jessica?"

Michael sighed. "She has been taken to Satan's realm through that door."

Liz directed her attention to the door Michael pointed at.

"Perhaps you should start from the beginning," Liz said.

"Perhaps I should," Michael replied.

Before he could say another word, Michael gave a strange look at the doors' entrance, catching the attention of the six people around him. The door opened and a young-looking man walked in. Their eyes met.

"Michael," the man said, "what are you doing here?"

John Walker, the oldest and, therefore, unofficial team captain of his circle of friends, was having a hard time, like everyone else, wrapping his head around the events that had just happened.

What was I thinking, ready to fight some mysterious guy and his cronies that appeared out of nowhere?

The truth was, all he was thinking about was he'd do the same thing for any one of his friends. It wasn't because he had anything to prove, he just loved his friends. When Michael had told them to all find a place to pray, he went into the closest room and shut the door. Like Michael had said he prayed for strength, guidance, wisdom, and to have patience.

He knew the old saying about praying for patience, "Don't pray for patience, God will make you learn it," or something to that effect, but he also knew he and his friends would also need it on the journey they faced together.

He also prayed for Jess. He didn't know what was going on beyond the door, but he knew it wasn't good for her.

"I don't know what she is facing in there, Lord," he prayed. *I don't even know what we will face in there.*

He prayed for her protection, and theirs. When John finished praying, he walked back to the door, but before he opened it, he heard what sounded like Mrs. Whites' voice.

Well, she's here, John thought. *Give her strength, Lord. Please.*

As John opened the door, he saw a stranger standing at the entrance. The stranger spoke.

"Michael, what are you doing here?"

Though John went off by himself to pray. Tim, Plate, and Bobby went into one room together to pray. Sarah, Ashley, and Maggie went into a different room, as well. Tim was the first to speak.

"Plate, I'm sorry for going off on you like that. I'm...I'm just really worried about Jess, that's all."

"Come here," Plate said, pulling Tim into a hug.

"It's no problem. I understand you're a bit upset. I know I can come off as a little bit of a goofball at times, but that's the way I deal with things. I didn't mean to upset you anymore back there. I'm sorry."

As the two backed away from their embrace, Tim asked, "So, how should we do this? Put three chairs in a circle, or stand and hold hands?"

"How about we kneel in prayer?" Bobby suggested.

"'A lot of kneeling puts you in good standing with God,'" Plate quoted. "I have that plaque in my bedroom."

"What about that other one?" Tim said.

"'The quickest way to God is your knees to the floor.' Or something like that."

"Something like that," Bobby replied. "So, do we agree on kneeling in prayer?"

Plate and Tim nodded in agreement.

As they got down on their knees, Plate asked, "Who wants to lead in prayer?"

"I think I'd like to," Tim replied.

As they bowed their heads, Tim started.

"Lord, um…You know I, um, pray better silently, but, uh…we come to You Lord, Bobby, Plate--er-- Paul-- I mean--"

Plate whispered in Tim's ear, "He knows our names. Relax."

"Anyway, Lord," Tim started again. "We come to You on behalf of our friend, Jessica. We, uh, pray for her safety. We pray for Your guidance and protection in what we are about to face."

Tim got quiet and Plate took the lead.

"Lord, we thank You for all You've given us and all the times You were with us, even if we didn't realize it at the time. We thank you for Your love and mercy. We pray You would watch over us in the coming conflict. The Bible says that where there are two or three gathered in Your name, there You will be also. We pray You would forgive us, Lord, of any sins that are in our lives. In Jesus' sweet and Holy name, we pray. Amen."

No one moved from where they were at. They prayed in silence, asking the Lord for His help, strength, wisdom, and love.

"Amen," Bobby said, raising.

"Amen," Tim and Plate repeated.

The three embraced.

"Whatever happens," Plate said, "it's in God's hands now."

"It's always been in God's hands," Bobby said.

"You're right," Plate replied.

As Tim walked over and opened the door, they heard a new voice in the main room, saying:

"What are you doing here?"

After the door was shut behind them, Ashley spoke up.

"Okay, okay, let's review. Jess has been kidnapped by Satan's goons, and Michael--*The Michael*--the Archangel is in the next room. Did I forget anything?"

"Quite a bit," Maggie said. "But thanks for the really abridged version."

"That's not funny," Ashley said.

"It wasn't supposed to be," Maggie said.

"The whole story is more like this: Satan had Jess kidnapped to destroy her soul using mankind's imagination; we have to go get her."

"Ashley, you know you just sounded like Plate and Tim, right?" Sarah asked.

"How is that?"

"The mix of sarcasm and attitude."

Ashley groaned.

"You're all scared," Maggie said. "This is a lot to take in all at once."

"You got that right," Sarah said.

"Let's pray," Maggie said taking Sarah's and Ashley's hands.

"Let's have silent prayer first. When you're done, squeeze my hand, then I'll pray out loud, okay."

The girls nodded.

"Okay," Maggie said, as they bowed their heads.

After a couple of moments, the girls squeezed Maggie's hands.

"Lord, we come to You on behalf of Jessica and ourselves. We pray for Your strength, guidance, mercy, and wisdom. Keep us safe in this time, as we go into the unknown. In the name above all names, the name of Jesus. Amen."

Maggie looked at Sarah, then at Ashley.

"Are you ready?"

Ashley looked at Sarah.

Sarah nodded.

"As ready as we'll ever be, I guess," Ashley replied.

"Then let's get back out there."

The three hugged then made their way to the door. As they opened it, they heard a voice say:

"...You doing here?"

CHAPTER SIX

As Stone walked his way around the Spiritual Realm, He was stopped by two demon Guards. One male, the other female.

"Halt!" the male demon said.

The male demon was green in color, and had a reptilian looking face, almost like a lizard.

"Proceed no further in the skin you're in," the female announced.

The female had the face of a human, though she was blue in color.

Stone smiled.

"Why?" He asked.

He knew the reason; he just wanted them to go through the trouble of explaining it.

"No flesh can abide here," the male lizard said.

"The flesh you carry with you will be destroyed," the female said.

"Why do you tell me this?" Stone asked.

"What do you care of human flesh?"

"It is not that we care," the male said.

"It is that you might desire to keep the flesh you have for a good while longer," the female replied.

"And where might I store my flesh for the time being?"

The male guard pointed with his axe toward a glass case.

"There! Step into the case; then it will be filled with a substance that will leave your host unconscious."

Stone walked up to the case and made his way in. As he stood inside, the substance filled the case. When it was well above his head, Stone--In demon form--moved out of his host and through the glass.

He stood there. Gargoyle-like features and stone-colored flesh, wings outstretched towering over the glass that held the human body.

"Ah," Stone said, "as good as the human flesh is for me and my brethren, it feels good to be free from it for a time."

Stone wrapped his wings around himself and turned to face the guards.

"Stonewraith!" the male demon with the axe said.

"You know the Rules of The Flesh. Why would you have us repeat them for you?"

"Ah, Corrupter, good to see you too," Stone said.

"What about me?" the female asked.

"Infidelity, always a pleasure, I'm sure." Infidelity smiled.

"So, where have you been all these years? And where did you pick up that specimen of flesh?" She asked as she looked at the host in the glass case.

"Easy, 'Deli,' you don't know where he's been," Stone replied.

"I don't think she cares, because you were controlling him," Corrupter said.

Stone laughed.

"I guess you're right there, Corrupter."

"Where have you been, Stonewraith?" Infidelity asked, ignoring their comments.

"I'm going by Stone for short right now," Stone said.

"I'm stationed in the Americas right now: North and South. I have been there for some time now. I'd say about fifty earth years now. How long have you two been posted here?"

"Not long," Corrupter said. "We have over 200 pairs stationed here. If we were not here, it would be no problem for someone else to be here."

"Interesting," Stone replied. "So, this isn't a demotion of some sort for a mission gone bad?"

"No, not for the two of us, anyway," Corrupter replied.

"How long have you used that host over there?" Infidelity asked, getting the topic back on Stone.

"Hmm... about forty years. I took him when he was a young man."

"What brings you here, now?" Corrupter asked.

"Information," Stone replied.

"Past or Present?" Infidelity asked.

Stone smiled. "Forbidden."

"Hmm, Lucifer usually comes to get that himself, or he sends some lower-level demon to retrieve something like that," Corrupter said. "Why are you here to get it?"

"Special assignment," Stone replied. "We are going to destroy a young woman's soul in a world of the human imaginations that Lucifer designed himself.

"I want to handle this information personally."

"Ooh...I want to be in! Can I come with you?" Infidelity asked.

Stone smiled. "Do you know of someone else who will help guard your post?"

"Go! Do what you need to do, and when you get back, I'll have someone here helping Corrupter guard our post and I'll be ready to go with you."

"Good enough. Corrupter, did you want to come too?" Stone asked.

"Nah, I'm fine here."

Stone looked at Infidelity and said, "I'll be right back."

"I'll be waiting," she said with a devilish grin.

"Stone, make a left on the last left turn and Forbidden is the last door on the left."

Stone smiled. "Thanks, Corrupter."

Stone walked his way through the labyrinth of halls and doors.

"What am I doing here?" Michael replied, "I could ask you the same thing!"

"Michael, do you know this guy?" Jeff asked.

Michael looked at Jeff and replied, "Yes."

"Okay..." Jeff said, "Who is he?"

"Theron. He is also one of the angels."

"Good to see you remember me after two millennia, Michael," Theron said while walking over to embrace him.

As the two angels embraced, Liz asked, "Is someone please going to explain to me what is going on here? Where's my Jessica? What is happening?"

At that time, Maggie and the youths made their way back to the rest of the group.

"Michael," Theron said, "what is going on here? I came here because I felt the presence of the Fallen. I only walked in here because I felt your presence."

Michael looked at Elizabeth and said, "Satan has come to the Throne of the Almighty God, seeking to make a world of his design, using the imagination of mankind. He has taken Jessica there in hopes of breaking her will and denying Christ as her Lord."

"Mercy!" Liz cried.

Michael continued. "The Almighty gave Satan permission, but he could not hurt her physically. He also told Satan that He would be sending a few of his Chosen to rescue her from his grasp."

"But why?" Liz pleaded. "Why Jessica?"

"Only the Almighty knows. This is not the first time Satan has come to the Throne of God and asked to harass someone, and it will not be the last."

"Until, at last, Satan is finally thrown into the Lake of Fire," Pastor Stevens added.

"Yes," Michael said.

Liz looked up at Michael and asked, "Could you explain the door again? Please?"

Michael looked at the door. "The door leads to the realm Satan has designed. Jessica was taken by a group called The Faithful. In this effort, they were led by a demon named Stone."

"Stone!" Theron said, "You mean Stonewraith?"

Michael looked at Theron. "Yes."

"You know him?" Pastor Stevens asked. "I mean, you all know each other. You all were angels together. Oh, boy," Stevens said, running his hands through his hair.

"You know what I mean, don't you?"

"Yes, I do," Theron said. "I faced him about five human Earth years ago, but he managed to escape me."

"Anyway," Michael said, turning his attention back to Liz. "Elizabeth, is there anything else you would like to know?"

"Well, um, who are these Chosen that are to rescue Jessica?"

"That would be us..." John said, motioning towards himself, Plate, Tim, Sarah, and Ashley.

Liz sucked in a breath. "God be with you."

"He always is," Pastor Stevens said.

Michael smiled. "It is now time."

The door swung open.

As Stone walked the halls, he would give casual glances at some of the words on the doors.

History on Earth... Dead languages... Forgotten lands... Uncharted galaxies...etc.

Other doors dealt with different countries, states, and cities, all the way down to neighborhoods. Some doors were for the history; other doors were to get there. Finally, Stone found the door he wanted: Forbidden.

"Ah, Forbidden," Stone said. "The place of darkest secrets."

Stone opened the door right into a mass of activity.

"Hey, watch it!" A gnome-like demon said, passing the opened door with a stack of papers clear over his head.

Stone walked in, closed the door, and looked around. The first thing he noticed was the computers. Lots and lots of computers. All hooked up to each other, yet somehow not tangled up. The next thing he noticed was the sea. The blackest, darkest sea Stone ever laid eyes on. The computers circled the sea.

"The Sea of Forgetfulness," Stone muttered.

"Quite a sight, ain't it? From a high view, it looks like an eye."

Stone looked for the voice and noticed the gnome-like demon standing next to him, the stack of papers gone.

"Spoil," Stone said. "It sure is. How long have you been here?"

"Three or four thousand years, give or take a couple hundred years."

Stone nodded. "This is the first time I've been here."

"Well, what brings ya by, Stonewraith?"

"I'm on assignment. I'm looking for Embellish, can you point me in the right direction?"

Spoil laughed.

"In this place? I might as well take you there myself."

"Lead the way. By the way, it's just Stone right now," Stone said.

"So noted," Spoil said.

As Spoil led Stone to Embellish, Stone noticed signs with bold gold lettering placed five feet from each other all around the inky Black Sea: **NO FISHING**.

Stone laughed.

"Is something funny?" Spoil asked.

"Those signs," Stone said, pointing.

Spoil looked at the signs and laughed as well. "Oh, yeah. He thinks a few signs are gonna stop us. It hasn't yet."

As they walked, a few of the other demons noticed Stone and acknowledged him; others were so engrossed with what they were doing, only Armageddon would unglue them from their chairs.

"Embellish!" Spoil yelled. "Ya got yourself a visitor!"

A hooded figure looked up from his workstation and said, "Must be Stonewraith. Or Stone for short at this time. Am I right?"

"Yes," Stone said.

"Well," Spoil said, "If ya don't need me anymore, I got stuff to do. Ya know, make sure the Devil is in the details."

Spoil laughed and walked away.

"Embellish, did Misery tell you what I needed?"

"He did," Embellish said, pulling out a device from his desk and tossing it to Stone.

"Everything you wanted to know about Jessica Rose White and some she wished you didn't. The device you have in your hand has her whole life, her 'Forgiven' thoughts and actions. It is connected to all these computers and is constantly updating."

"That's great. Now, what about her friends? I need stuff on them, too."

"Like I said, the device is always updating, all you have to do is type in a name, and it will be uploaded to you."

Stone smiled evilly. "Perfect."

"Will that be all?" Embellish asked.

Stone looked around then said, "One more thing."

"I'm listening," he said, folding his arms.

"How does all this work?" Stone said waving his hand around the computers and the Sea.

"Well, originally we would put nets into the Sea and file the contents by hand. Now, we have these computers and a specialized net that we attached around the 'Waterfall,' if you will, to receive the information, transferring the data directly to our mainframe of computers. It has made our work here so much easier in the past twenty years to have it. We are about fifty percent done with our filing."

"Fifty?" Stone asked.

"Well, you see, after one of the humans dies, we aren't as enthusiastic about retrieving the information. Yes, we still collect it, but at a slower pace since it isn't...as needful as others."

"I see; tell me more about this 'Waterfall' you mentioned."

"Ah, yes. The source of all this delightful information. It is right over here. It comes out of thin air. No entrance and no exit; it just flows."

"Amazing," Stone said. "Do you know where it comes from?"

"Researchers are still puzzled at that. They have no idea."

"Hmm...Interesting," Stone said. "Now that I have what I need, I will be on my way. Keep up the good work, Embellish."

"I do what I can," Embellish said.

Trisha walked the halls of the complex, careful not to get lost. She decided that since it was a huge place, she would start by making only left turns, which is why when she wanted to get back, all she had to do was make right turns. There wasn't much to see, though she would stop at a window and look out.

"Weird," she said. "Everything has a reddish tinge to it, except the monsters out there."

Trish had never seen creatures like that before, only in the movies, and in some graphic novels she would look at.

"Trish! Trish!" someone called for her.

Trisha looked around.

"Travis," Trisha said.

Travis came running up to her.

"Trish! This place is amazing! Some of the guys have found, like, a control room for the outside. We can create our own characters and control, like, three or four of them at once. We can even control some of the monsters out there!"

"That's great. Aren't you worried about getting lost in this place?"

Travis looked puzzled, then laughed.

"No, not really," Travis touched the crystal necklace and said, "The crystal seems to work as a beacon. If I wanted to get back, it would lead the way. That's how I found you. It led me to you."

"Really?" Trisha said.

"I ain't lying."

"Looks like this little crystal is more than meets the eye, huh?"

"You got that right. Like I said, this place is awesome! I think I'll go back to the outside control room. You can come by when you want, just have your crystal lead you."

Trisha smiled as he ran around the corner. Trisha looked down and touched her crystal necklace.

"What else can you do?" she wondered aloud.

The music—if you could call it that—stopped.

"Oh, thank You, Lord," Jess prayed.

Jess had no idea how long that noise was on for, but it felt like an eternity.

She removed the pillow that she was using to muffle most of the "music" out from over her face and sat upright on the cot.

"What's the matter? You don't like my song choice?"

Jess looked at the speaker, then the mirror. She didn't recognize the voice. It wasn't that Stone guy. She was sure of that. It sounded like a younger voice, possibly a girl.

"You wouldn't have anything in the genre of Country, by any chance, would you?" Jess responded.

"Nope, all out," the voice from the speaker said.

"Who are you? What happened to Stone?"

"Oh, he stepped out for a moment. As for me, you don't need to know who I am right now."

"So, what? I just call you 'Voice Number 2,' is that it?"

The voice laughed.

"This brave act of yours is really funny. Okay, okay. You may call me Kim if you really need a name."

"Is that your real name?"

"Sort of," the voice called Kim replied.

Jess laid back on the cot and said, "I'm not even going to ask what that means."

"That is a wise choice at the moment."

"Hey, I'm thirsty. Will you let me have something to drink?"

No response.

Jess got off her cot, walked up to the mirror, and gave a light knock.

"Hello? I know you can see me and hear me! Can I have some water?"

Jess heard a rumbling and noticed in the mirror that something behind her was moving. She turned around to see something box-like coming from out of the wall. Jess walked up to the new addition of the room and noticed a handle on one of the three sides. Jess grabbed the handle and opened the door. Inside was a small bathroom.

"Satisfied?" Kim asked.

"The only thing missing is the shower," Jess retorted.

"Beggars can't be choosers. You should have made your reservations well in advance."

"Your humor is worse than my sarcasm," Jess replied.

"That's a matter of opinion, my dear."

Jess turned on the water and cupped her hands to drink.

"At least the water isn't red like outside," she commented.

"The water outside and in are the same. It poses no risk to you," Kim said.

"Lovely," Jess said walking out of the small restroom.

"How do I know if what you say is true?"

"We are forbidden to kill you."

Jess froze.

We are forbidden to kill you.

"You can't kill me?"

"That does not mean we can't make you miserable."

Before Jess could ask what she meant, she heard a bloodcurdling scream. Jess looked behind her to see a half-dressed, transparent girl running from a blood-soaked, transparent, masked man chasing after her.

"Enjoy the show. I do like watching these movies in holographic form, just as I'm sure you will."

Jess felt a wave of nausea again, just like when they first played the "music," but this time she couldn't fight it. Jess ran into the bathroom, thanking God that the contents of her stomach had a place to go.

CHAPTER SEVEN

As the door swung open, Maggie asked Peter, Liz, Julie, and Jack, "Would you guys help me with something?"

"What do you need?" Jack asked, looking at the door.

"Follow me," Maggie said.

"Come on, Liz, let's go," Jack said.

Liz silently obeyed.

"Peter, could you grab the box of those new Bibles and follow me, please?" Maggie asked.

"Yeah, sure, I guess," Peter replied.

"Maggie, what is this all about?" Jack asked.

"What's going on?"

"Hang on, Jack," Maggie said.

Maggie led them to her office.

"Sit the box down on my desk, please, Peter."

Peter sat the box down and asked, "What's up, Maggie?"

Maggie looked around the room and sighed.

"Look, guys. Right now, I don't think there is anything else we can do right now except pray. So, I thought we could do something productive while we pray."

"Okay..." Jack said.

Maggie turned to the box on her desk and pulled out a small device.

"Jeff and I asked a local company if they could make an easy-to-use electric Bible with enough room for a variety of different downloads. They were able to do so."

"I'm sorry but get to the point!" Liz said.

Jack put his arm around Liz. "We'll get her back, Liz. Even if I have to go in there myself with a tank to do it."

"Maybe this wasn't a good idea," Maggie said, looking up at the ceiling.

"Go ahead," Jack said, "We're listening."

"I was thinking that we could each grab a Bible and download the needed information onto it. It wouldn't be that hard. I have all the different links and computer downloads in a folder on my computer."

"So, you've got one already done?" Jack said.

"Yeah, I spent some time on it," Maggie said. "In fact, it should be right here..."

Maggie started taking the devices out of the box.

"Hmm..." Maggie said. "Peter, were there any of these left on the table?"

Peter thought for a second.

"No, I put them all back in the box. Why?"

"I seem to be missing the one I used. I thought I put it back in the box earlier. Anyway..."

Maggie said going to the computer, "All you need to do is attach this cable to the Bible."

Maggie hooked the device to the computer, using a USB port on the side.

"Then you turn on the Bible. As you can see, it's small, but you can see the screen perfectly..."

Maggie stopped talking and had a strange look on her face.

"Maggie? What's up?" Peter asked.

"Jess said the same thing!" Maggie said.

"What?" Julie asked.

Maggie looked at Jack, Liz, and Julie.

"Jess said the same thing about seeing the screen perfectly..."

"Just before she put it in her pocket," Peter finished.

"That's right!" Maggie said, standing up.

Maggie grabbed Liz's hand.

"Do you know what that means?"

"I'm in too much shock, dear," Liz said.

"You're gonna have to spell it out for me."

Maggie smiled.

"It means she is armed with the Truth of God's word."

"Oh!" Liz cried. "Thank God!"

"Now, I'm not sure if anything else will work, but the main Bible came standard on it, so it should work."

"Thank you, Lord," Jack said.

Maggie looked at Peter.

"Peter, do you think you could download the Bible that's already hooked up? The file name is 'Bible Downloads.' It's all there."

"Sure! What are you going to do?" Peter asked.

"I'm going to tell Jeff that Jess has one of the Bibles.

"I'll be right back."

The group walked through the door.

"Hey," Tim said. "Where are we? It just looks like another room in the church Rec center."

"Except for all the gadgets," Plate said.

The room was filled with all sorts of things. From gadgets on tables, to what looked like weapons hanging on the walls, to a couple of computer workstations in a corner of the room.

"Here, you will choose what you will take with you," Michael said. "If you do not find what you need, you may use the computers over there to design what you need. It also has a catalog of things not in this room."

"You mean there is more stuff than this?" Sarah asked.

"Yes, there are vehicles, suits of armor, and other things. Remember, you are entering a world of imagination. You humans have come up with a lot of interesting things using your imaginations over these many years."

"Great," Sarah said. "We have no idea what we are getting into."

"Well, you know what the Boy Scouts say," Jeff said walking in. "'Always be prepared.' A true statement, I must say."

Ring. Ring.

"That's me," Ashley said, grabbing her cell phone and checking the Caller ID.

Ring. Ring.

She looked at Tim and said, "It's our parents."

"Answer it," Tim said. "Put it on speaker."

Ring. Ring.

As Tim and Ashley walked out of the room, she put her cell on speaker.

"Hello?" Ashley said.

"Hey, Honey," her father, Bradley Cook said.

"Hey, Sweetheart," Jillian Cook said.

Ashley and Tim exchanged glances.

"What's up, guys? How's the honeymoon?" Ashley asked.

There was silence on the other end.

"Mom, Dad?" Ashley asked.

"Is everything okay there?" Jill asked, worry in her voice.

Tim and Ashley looked at each other.

"There's something wrong, isn't there?" Brad asked.

"Yes," Ashley said.

"What is it? What's wrong?" Jill asked.

Ashley looked over at Michael and mouthed, "What do I say?"

"The truth," Michael said softly.

"Ashley? Timothy?" Jill asked.

"Mom," Tim said, "Satan has attacked Jess."

"Oh, Lord," Jill said.

"The Holy Spirit told us something was amiss," Brad said.

"Mom, Dad," Ashley said, "Just pray for Jess, okay? We'll tell you more when you come home."

"Okay," Brad said. "Tell Jess we love her, and we are praying for her."

Ashley looked at Tim. "Okay, we will."

"We love both of you, too," Jill said.

"We love you, too," Tim said.

"Bye, guys," Brad said.

"Bye," Ashley said.

As Ashley hung up, Tim asked, "How are we going to explain this to them when they get back?"

"Do not worry about that right now," Michael said.

Ashley looked at her cell as she walked back into the room.

"I think it would be a good idea if we left our phones and other items here."

"Good idea, Ash," Tim said. "We don't want to end up losing anything in there."

Everyone agreed and placed their belongings on a vacant spot at one of the computer workstations.

"Well, then," John said once his pockets were empty. "Where do we start?"

"Start where you think is best and move from there," Theron said.

John looked at Theron.

"Theron, can you tell us about yourself? You said you haven't seen Michael in two thousand years. Is that common among angels? Not to see each other for so long?"

Theron looked at Michael. "Have I got time to tell them?"

"That is fine with me. I don't even know what you have been up to. I was never briefed on your case."

"You don't know what he's been doing?" Plate asked.

"I might be an Archangel but that does not mean I must know everything. The Almighty tells me what I need to know when I need to know it."

"Then would God want you to tell us what you've been doing, Theron?" Tim asked.

"The Almighty has made it possible for Michael and I to cross paths once again. If I were not allowed to say, I would not have been put here with you all."

"Good point," Jeff said.

"Shall I start, then?" Theron asked Michael.

"Please," Michael said.

"It started when our Lord came home..."

A trumpet sounds.

"Glory! Glory! Glory!" the Angels announced. "Our Lord has redeemed the Earth with His Blood and has returned to sit at the Almighty's right hand!"

Thunderous applause from both Angels and humans erupted throughout Heaven.

"Holy! Holy! Holy! Is the Lamb that was slain for the sins of man!"

Jesus raised His arms, exposing His nail-scared wrists.

The crowd quieted.

"I carry these scars so that mankind will know what I have done for them. I paid the penalty. Now the only thing the inhabitants of the Earth must do is accept Me, as both their Lord God and their personal Savior. No longer must they make animal sacrifices to atone for their sins. I, the Son of the Most High God, was slain so they might live with Me. I have become the Ultimate Sacrifice!"

The crowd cheered again and began singing praises in honor of their Lord.

"Avdeel!" Jesus spoke. "Meet with me."

"Yes, my Lord!" Avdeel said.

"Theron," Avdeel said a short while later.

"Yes, Avdeel?" Theron said.

"The Lord has a mission for you."

"I will go where He commands," Theron replied.

"What will He have me do, Avdeel?"

"He wants you on the Earth, banishing a great number of the Fallen to the Pit until the appointed time," Avdeel replied.

"Just me?" Theron asked.

"There are others. They will be revealed in time."

"I understand. I will not fail my Lord. When do I leave?"

"Now," Avdeel said. "Godspeed, my brother."

"Thank you, brother."

"Whoa!" Plate said. "You mean you're a demon hunter?"

"Yes, although there are some demons who have escaped my grasp from time to time."

"Like Stone?" Tim asked.

"Yes, and others."

"So do you know how many demon hunters there are?" Ashley asked.

"I am still not sure. I have come across a few others. It has taken two or more of us together to send some demons to the Pit."

"The Pit," John said. "You mean the Pit mentioned in Revelation? The Pit that will be opened to lose the demons during the tribulation judgments?"

"Yes," Theron said.

"I think this is a bit much to take in at once," John said.

"Jeff! Jeff!" Maggie came running into the room, all excited. Maggie looked around the room.

"Nice room," she commented.

"Maggie? What's up?"

Maggie's smile wouldn't fade.

"You know the Bibles we had made for the kids?"

"Yeah?"

"Well, Jess still has it."

Jeff gave a blank look.

"Slow down, Maggie, I'm not following," Jeff said.

"Okay, Jess has the Bible I worked on. I downloaded every Bible there was, even the audio Bibles, and some games from the internet. Downloaded the messenger and it has video networking. She has the fully useable Bible!"

It finally registered.

"All right!" Jeff said, hugging Maggie and twirling her around.

"What does that mean?" Tim asked.

"It means that Jess is not without help. Even if the messenger and video don't work, she has a Bible with her," Maggie said. "She is still equipped with the Word of God!"

"If they haven't taken it away," Tim replied.

"Have faith," John said, putting his hand on Tim's shoulder.

"I'll be right back," Maggie said. "I got Peter, Julie, Jack, and Liz trying to figure out how to update the rest. It'll take a while. I'm just trying to keep them occupied for a while. Give them something to do."

"Jeff," Pastor Stevens said. "Can you start at the beginning? What Bible?"

"Okay, okay," Jeff said. "Maggie and I asked a software computer company if they could make a specialized Bible, with study help and all sorts of other things. It would work like a Palm Pilot, Blackberry, and other things that are out now. Anyway, they made ten of them and sent us eight, free of charge. Maggie has been fiddling around with one of them to make sure it works. Jess must have been given that one. It also connects wirelessly to the internet, much like a cell phone, only you don't have to make any payments to use it after you purchase one."

"Free internet? I'm in," Plate said.

"You'll get yours once Maggie is done with them," Jeff said.

"Sounds good," Plate replied.

"The five of you may find what you think you will need," Michael said, motioning to the five youths.

"But first, come, stand in front of me."

John, Plate, Tim, Sarah, and Ashley did as they were asked.

Michael turned to Jeff and said, "Jeff, you have been preparing a lesson on the Armor of God."

"Yes, I am," Jeff responded. "But it is not finished."

"I want you to get your notes and share it with them."

Jeff looked at the youths, then looked back at Michael and sighed.

"Ok," he said. "I'll be right back."

Michael turned his attention back to the youths.

"I know you are familiar with the Armor of God, but I want you to look at it again. In a battle against Satan or his demons, you must be prepared to fight at any time. Like a soldier who sleeps with his gun in hand, ready to fight if need be. You must be ready."

Jeff came back carrying a couple of pieces of paper.

"I have it," Jeff said holding the papers in the air.

"Good," Michael said. "Now, read it out loud."

Jeff looked at the five youths standing before Michael and said, "I just started putting this lesson together this past week when I had time, bear with me. I don't like sharing any unfinished work with anyone except Pastor Stevens."

"And I haven't even seen it yet," Pastor Stevens replied, smiling.

"Yeah, well anyway," Jeff said. "Let me start out by reading from Ephesians 6:13-17:

'Stand, therefore, having your loins girt about with truth, and having on the breastplate of righteousness;
And your feet shod with the preparation of the gospel of peace;
Above all, taking the shield of faith, wherewith ye shall be able to quench all the fiery darts of the wicked.
And take the helmet of salvation, and the sword of the Spirit, which is the word of God.'"

"I then broke it down so it could be understood better.

Keep the Truth center in your life, protecting your heart from immorality, having faith that God will protect you with His undying love from anything Satan wants to throw at you. Standing firm with the indisputable fact of the freedom from sin that comes from Christ. Having your head protected from the thoughts of temptation and the sins you were delivered from and using God's word, with the help of the Holy Ghost, to combat the lies of Satan."

"That's pretty good," Tim said.

"Thanks, I'm not done yet," Jeff said smiling. "*God does not need armor, so it is safe to say it is the armor made by God. Or, the armor is of God, so we could say, put on the protection of God.* Sound good so far?" Jeff asked Michael.

"If it didn't, The Almighty wouldn't be having me have you read it."

"Good point," Jeff said. "Now, let's break it down:

Belt of Truth:

Speak honestly, lovingly, without sarcasm, and without emptiness of meaning, always."

"Or we can look at it another way:

Belt of Truth:
The truth is that God is one God with Three Persons:
Father, Son, and Holy Spirit. We are not perfect, but The Father loves us anyway, which is why He sent His Son to die for us, so we wouldn't have to go to Hell and be separated from His love. The Holy Spirit helps us in realizing the truth of God's love. We must speak the truth, always."

Jeff looked up. "How am I doing so far?"
"Good," John said. "We are to keep The Truth center, so everything falls into place."
"Because The Truth holds everything together," Ashley replied.
"Right," Jeff said. "Moving along:

Breastplate of Righteousness:
Through the Righteousness & Faith in Jesus, let us stand, having Him guard our hearts from hate, jealousy, and unforgiveness, knowing it is not our power, but Jesus who can protect our hearts, to stand against the devil and his army."

"Another way of looking at it:

Breastplate of Righteousness:
The righteousness that comes only from Christ. He is the only One who lived a perfect life. We need Him to help us and protect our hearts from evil."

"We need Christ's help to keep our hearts pure," Tim said.
Jeff smiled and continued to read:

"The Preparation of the Gospel of Peace:
Stay grounded in the Word of God. Study daily, so you won't be cornered

with questions you cannot answer. Always be prepared for things you don't see coming so you can stand firm no matter how rocky the terrain is."

"And another way is:

The Preparation of the Gospel of Peace:
By studying God's word, The Holy Bible, we can unearth the simple Truths God wants us to know, giving us the wisdom and knowledge on how to answer how and why we believe. Be ready to stand for what you believe."

"Like wearing the right shoes for the right time. You can stand better on rocks if you wear shoes instead of going barefoot," Plate said.

"Perfect example," Jeff said. "We need to stand on the Truth of God's word so we won't stumble at any time."

"Shield of Faith:
Know that Satan will attack you in any way he can. If he can't hit you directly, he will do it any other way he can. Stay strong in the faith, believing in God for the protection that is needed to continue in your stand against Satan."

"Another way is:

Shield of Faith:
Hebrews 11:1, "Now faith is the substance of things hoped for, the evidence of things not seen." Hope is belief or trust. Faith is the substance of trust in God. Trust that God can shield us from anything."

"Our shield is the promise of God's protection so long as we continue to have faith in Him?" Ashley asked.

"Yes," Jeff said. "Mind you, this lesson is still a work in progress."

Ashley nodded.

"Okay, now the next one:

The Helmet of Salvation:
Protect your minds with the Truth of God's Word. Remember, you have
a greater Hope in the Lord God than you do in this world. Do not let
anything distract you mentally, be it fear, doubt, or hopelessness. Give it
to God and He will lift that burden."

"Or:

The Helmet of Salvation:
Knowing that Christ saved you, even if sometimes you don't feel saved.
God will not leave you or forsake you. Even if you turn your back
on God,
He is there, with His arms open wide, ready to receive you once again."

"Keeping our minds on Christ will keep our thoughts from straying from God," John summarized. "But, even if we do, like the prodigal son, He will welcome us back."

Jeff nodded and moved to the last one:

"The Sword of The Spirit:
You cannot fight the devil and his armies with man-made weapons. You
must use the Word of God to advance against the enemy. The Word of
God is more powerful than Satan, his armies, and his weapons. The
Holy Spirit can and will help you with the Words you need to use. All
you have to do is be prayerfully open to Him and ready to listen."

"Here's something else that will help:

The Sword of The Spirit:
When Jesus was in the wilderness, being tempted by Satan, Jesus used
the Scriptures against him.

Hebrews 4:12 says, "For the word of God is quick, and powerful, and
sharper than any two-edged sword, piercing even to the dividing
asunder of soul and spirit, and of the joints and marrow, and is a
discerner of the thoughts and intents of the heart."

Against Satan, you must fight with the Word of God.
The Holy Spirit will give you the words needed."

"Only the Word of God and the name of Jesus can be used against Satan," Sarah said.

"Yes," Jeff said. "I have one more thing to add to all this:

"Only with the help of The Godhead or Trinity can you use the full Armor.

Just the Helmet and the Shield may help, but leaves you open in too many places.

A SWAT team member does not go in with only a shield and a helmet. He carries his weapon, a Kevlar vest, and protective boots, he is also well-trained and has studied his training manual.

Training Manual the belt of truth? The Bible is our training manual. Breastplate his Kevlar vest? His protective boots the shoes ready to stand? The SWAT shield to keep the fiery bullets from harming him? The helmet to protect his head from serious injury? His weapon, his gun, his own sword for combating evil?"

"Wow, Jeff," Plate said. "Great referencing of the Armor of God to SWAT gear."

"Thanks," Jeff said. "But as you can see, it has some rough edges that need to be smoothed out."

"It is just what they needed to hear," Michael said.

"Jeff," Tim said. "Could you repeat your version of the Armor? I'd like to hear it again."

"Sure," Jeff replied.

"Keep the Truth center in your life, protecting your heart from immorality, having faith God will protect you with His undying love from anything Satan wants to throw at you. Standing firm with the indisputable fact of the

freedom from sin that comes from Christ, having your head protected from the thoughts of temptation and the sins you were delivered from, and using God's Word, with the help of the Holy Ghost, to combat the lies of Satan."

"Now that is powerful," Tim said.

"Thanks, Tim," Jeff said.

Pastor Stevens put his hand on Jeff's shoulder and said, "Only God could have inspired you to write something like that. I'm proud of you."

Jeff smiled. "Thanks, Pastor."

"Now," Michael said. "You may now search for what you need for the physical fighting. Remember this: Satan will use anything to hinder you."

The five searched the room looking for what they might need.

"Will they be alright?" Jeff asked Michael.

"Only the Almighty knows that. I have been given the authority to use as many other angels as I need. They will join us once we are in Satan's Realm. I will also have Theron at my side to help these young warriors."

"Where are the other angels going to be?" Jeff asked.

"They scattered about the Realm, ready to fight when needed."

"How many angels are there?" Pastor Stevens asked.

"Enough," Michael said.

"Cool!" Plate said from across the room.

"Hey, guys! Check this out."

Plate held up a handle and pressed a switch.

"It's a laser sword. And look at this: when I change the settings, it becomes a laser whip!"

"Don't try that in here," John said. "You might hurt someone."

Plate shut it off.

"I think I'll take it," Plate said, attaching it to his belt loop.

"You find anything cool over there, Ashley?"

"I think so," Ashley replied holding up a crossbow.

"As far as I can tell, it has unlimited arrows."

"How can you tell that?" Plate asked.

Ashley stifled a laugh. "Because it says, 'Unlimited arrows' on the side."

"That's human imagination for ya," John said.

"You find anything yet, John?" Plate asked.

"Just some armor so far. What about you, Tim?"

"Nothing out here, so I'm checking the catalog. You wouldn't believe the things in here."

Tim seemed to think over his comment over for a second then said, "Then again, maybe you would."

"Okay, then," Plate said. "Sarah, is there anything interesting over there?"

"You tell me," Sarah said, wearing a fiery red body suit, with a shield in her hand.

"Wow, Sarah," John said. "Where's your weapon?"

"I'm wearing it," Sarah replied.

"Really?"

"Yeah, watch this."

The shield that was in her hand slowly became one with her body suit, and in her other hand, a sword emerged.

"Unbelievable," Pastor Stevens said.

"Wow," Jeff added.

"You got that right," Sarah said with a laugh.

"I guess I'm ready."

"Me, too," Plate said, holding a shield, a staff, and wearing a brown-colored breastplate.

"I found four other swords/whips, I have a shield and staff. And the breastplate holds a couple of nun chucks at the sides."

"Two down, three to go," Theron said.

"Make that two to go," Ashley said, wearing a black hooded cloak with a crossbow in each hand.

"You look like the Grim Reaper," Plate said.

Theron laughed.

Plate looked at Theron.

"The Grim Reaper does look like that, right?"

Theron looked at Michael, then back to Plate.

"I'm staying out of this one, kid."

"You don't like the color, Plate? Fine. How about this?"

The color of the cloak turned green, then blue, then yellow.

"You like it now?" Ashley asked, sweetly.

"Holy cow!" Plate said.

He then looked at Michael and Theron.

"Sorry," he muttered.

"Tim, John," Jeff said. "Are you guys almost done?"

"I need a few more minutes," Tim said.

"I think so," John said wearing a gold-plated body suit with a ski mask, holding a spiked shield in one hand, a sword in the other.

"Looks like C-3PO meets Jason," laughed Plate.

"'I am fluent in over five million languages.' Yeah, maybe, Plate. Just maybe," John said.

Bobby walked and took a look around.

"Cool," he said.

"Hey, Jeff," Tim said. "Is it okay if Bobby grabs your digital music player? I have an idea."

Jeff looked at Tim.

"I guess so, Bobby, in my office, under the window, there is what looks like a computer tower. It's about half the size of a regular computer. Could you get it for me?"

"Sure!" Bobby said, leaving.

"What are you thinking, Tim?" Jeff asked.

"Well, it's kind of hard to explain. I was thinking I could download the music into the suit I'm making. The suit should be able to make speakers that could go up in the air and just hover there. I could have it play whatever music I want from them."

Jeff looked at him.

"And just what kind of suit are you making?"

"You'll see," Tim said.

Before Jeff could make a comment, Bobby came rushing in.

"Is this it?" He asked.

Tim looked at Bobby. "Yeah, bring it over."

As Tim was connecting it to the computer, Jeff said, "It might take a while to download, I have thousands of songs on there. From old hymns, praise and worship, to children's songs--"

"Done!" Tim said.

"Well, I'll be," Jeff said. "You downloaded all the songs? That quick?"

"Yeah," Tim said unhooking the DMP from the computer.

"You can take it back now, Bobby, thanks."

As Bobby took it back, Tim read the screen.

"Okay...When finished, press 'Enter.' To abort, press 'Esc'. Well, I guess I'm finished. Here goes nothing."

Tim pressed the "Enter" button.

Suddenly, a white light surrounded Tim.

"Tim!" Ashley yelled.

Michael placed a hand on her shoulder.

"He is fine," the Archangel said.

The light vanished.

There stood Tim, encased in a robotic suit.

"Uh...this must be how Darth Vader felt like," Tim said.

"Except, you can feel all your limbs, right?" Plate asked.

"Yeah, I can," Tim replied. "Hey, check this out."

Out of the back of Tim's hands came three four-inch-long blades.

"Whoa, cool!" Plate said.

"I think they can get longer, but I don't want to try it in here."

"Good idea," Pastor Stevens said.

"Well," John said, "I think we are all ready. What now?"

"Prayer," Pastor Stevens said.

"I'll get the others," Jeff said.

"Do you think we're ready Michael?" John asked.

"So long as you understand that not everything you face there can be defeated with physical weapons."

"I--" John looked around the room, facing his friends.

They all nodded.

"We understand."

"Good," Michael said.

Jeff came back with Maggie, Jack, Julie, Liz, and Bobby with Lex walking beside him.

"Hey," Tim said, "where has Lex been?"

"I guess he's been laying by the side door all this time," Bobby said.

Pastor Stevens looked around.

"Where's Peter?" He asked.

"He had to get back to work," Maggie said.

"He wanted to stay. I told him there wasn't anything left here he could do except pray. He told me he would be praying hard."

"As well we all should," Pastor Stevens said.

"Let's all join hands," Jeff said. "Pastor, would you lead us in prayer?"

"Lord God, we come to You in prayer. We asked that You protect Jessica. We asked that the Bible she has with her will act as a lifeline, in the mists of a dark sea, ready to drown her. Father, watch over these five young ones. Give them the faith to overcome whatever they are to face, in the lair of the enemy. We ask You for their protection as well. In the Name of Jesus, which is above all other names, Amen."

"Amen!" The rest said in unison.

"Please," Liz said. "Bring back my Jessica."

"Continue praying," Michael said as he opened up a hidden door against the wall.

Lex dashed for the door.

Theron stepped in the dog's path.

"Hold it there, little doggie. I don't really think it's such a good idea for you to be coming with us right now. It might get a little dangerous."

Lex tilted his head.

"I think he understands," Bobby said, retrieving his dog.

Michael smiled, then looked at Liz, and said, "Remember: Great is His faithfulness."

"Great is His faithfulness..." Liz whispered.

Then, as the five humans and two Angels went through the door, Liz started singing.

"Great is Thy faithfulness..."

One by one, the remaining people joined in:

Great is thy faithfulness, O God my Father!

There is no shadow of turning with Thee;
Thou changest not, Thy compassions, they fail not:
As Thou hast been, Thou forever wilt be.

Great is Thy faithfulness, Great is Thy faithfulness,
morning by morning new mercies I see;
All I have needed Thy hand hath provided—
Great is Thy faithfulness, Lord, unto me!

Summer and winter, and spring-time and harvest,
Sun, moon, and stars in their courses above,
join with all nature in manifold witness
To Thy great faithfulness, mercy, and love.

Great is Thy faithfulness, Great is Thy faithfulness,
morning by morning new mercies I see;
All I have needed Thy hand hath provided—
Great is Thy faithfulness, Lord, unto me!

Pardon for sin and a peace that endureth,
Thine own dear presence to cheer and to guide,
Strength for today and bright hope for tomorrow—
Blessings all mine, with ten thousand beside!

Great is Thy faithfulness, Great is Thy faithfulness,
morning by morning new mercies I see;
All I have needed Thy hand hath provided—
Great is Thy faithfulness, Lord, unto me! Amen.

"Lord," Jeff prayed, "we know Your faithfulness is Great... Watch over these young people, Lord. You alone are worthy of praise. We praise You for all that You have done in their lives and what You will do also. Show them Your love. We ask again for the protection of Jessica. Watch over her. In Your Word it says where two or three are gathered in Your name, You are in the mists. We pray You will be with us. I pray a special blessing, Lord, for our dear sister, Elizabeth, Lord. I know this can't be easy for her. I don't entirely know what she is feeling, but I know, Lord, You do. Amen.

Crying, Liz wrapped her arms around Jeff.

"Thank you," she whispered.

CHAPTER EIGHT

Trisha walked back into the control room.

"Did I miss anything?" she asked.

"Not much," Kim replied.

Trisha looked through the mirror and asked, "Are those holograms in there?"

"Yes! Pretty cool, huh?"

"I guess. Where's Jessica? What's that wall at the head of the bed?"

"The extra wall is a small restroom. She's been trying to hide from the screams and carnage of the holograms."

Trisha laughed.

"Let me guess. No such luck."

"She can't hide from the screams."

Before Trisha could say another word, someone else said, "Honey, I'm home."

Trisha turned around to see Mr. Stone and a beautiful, blue-colored woman.

Trisha blinked.

"Miss Conner. May I introduce a colleague of mine?"

Miss Conner? Trisha thought.

"I never told you my last name."

Stone put his sunglasses on and said, "We have the same master, remember? He gave me your last name."

"Oh, yeah," Trisha said.

"Anyway," Stone said. "Miss Trisha Conner, this is my colleague, Infidelity."

"You can call me Deli if you like," Infidelity said.

"Okay...Deli. This is my sister Kim."

"I know. I was briefed on the way here."

Trisha felt uneasy but shook it off.

"What have I missed?" Stone asked.

"I-I don't know. I was looking around. You'll have to ask Kim."

Stone looked at Kim.

"Well?"

"I played the music for a while. Then I decided to use the holograms. I also unlocked the secret restroom."

"Ah! Good. No reason to deny the most basic of human needs."

"She's been hiding in there for a while."

"She won't be for long, I'm sure."

Stone then looked at Trisha.

"Tell me, Miss Conner. Find anything fascinating while you were looking around?"

"One of my men came to me and said they had found a control room for the outside."

"Very good," Stone said. "How about you and your...sister take a better look around?"

Taking the hint, Trisha said, "Come on, Kim. Let's take a look around."

Kim followed Trisha out of the room.

After the two had left, Stone went to the control panel and shut the hologram off.

Then he spoke into the microphone, "Come out, come out wherever you are."

Stone laughed into the microphone.

"Don't tell me you're sleeping? I promise you a short break from the music and the holograms."

"Yeah," Jess' voice answered. "Bet your word is your bond, right?"

Stone laughed again.

"Not really. But you can believe me on this."

Still nothing.

"Look," Stone said. "That bathroom of yours does provide privacy for you. You have three options:

A. You can come out of there on your own.

B. I can have someone, or something remove you from there.

or C. I can press a button and remove that bathroom of yours and you don't get it back.

How does that sound? Whatever you choose, you are coming out of there. Do you understand? You have thirty seconds to decide. 30...29...28...27..."

———

Jess knew she didn't have much of a choice.

"...26...25...24..." Stone continued on.

She didn't want anything physically removing her from her resting place, and she surely didn't want the tiny restroom removed.

"...23...22...21..."

Though it didn't block out the horrific screams, it muffled it some. But not much.

"...20...19...18..."

Jess opened the door.

"All right," Jess said, stepping out and looking at the mirror.

"You win. Are you happy now?"

"For the moment," the speaker said.

"What do you people want with me?"

"Take a look out your window," Stone said.

"You didn't answer me."

"Look out your window," Stone said again.

"Fine," Jess said, glaring at the mirror.

Jess walked over to the window.

All she saw was flying creatures in the air and all other sorts of creatures on the ground.

"And just what am I supposed to be seeing?"

"Look straight ahead," Stone replied.

Jess looked back, taking a few steps to the mirror.

"I am. What am I supposed to be seeing?"

"Look straight ahead."

Jess walked back to the mirror.

"What is going on? Why am I here?"

"Miss White, I suggest you look out the window before I make you."

Jess opened up her mouth to say something but thought better of it.

She turned around and looked out the window.

"That's better," Stone said. "Tell me, what do you see in the air?"

"A bunch of monsters," Jess replied.

"Good, good. Look straight ahead and tell me what you see."

Jess looked straight ahead.

"I see... a red... dragon, it looks like."

"Good. Watch that."

Jess turned her head back to the mirror.

"Are you serious?" Jess asked.

"Deadly," Stone replied.

Jess swallowed and looked at the dragon.

"The dragon seems to be getting closer," Jess said.

"Good."

Jess studied the dragon as it got closer.

And closer...

And closer...

It's gonna hit the building! Jess thought.

Jess ran to the farthest corner of the window and braced for impact.

CHAPTER NINE

Nothing happened.

No collision.

No earth-shattering explosion.

"Hello, Jessica," a man's voice said.

Jess knew the new voice didn't come from the speaker in the other corner. It was too clear.

Jess looked around the room.

A man stood in the room with Jess.

He was well-built. About average height, neatly cut brown hair, trimmed mustache and beard, and wearing an expensive-looking tuxedo.

Very handsome.

Shocked by her thought, Jess asked, "Who are you?"

"Who do you think I am?" the man asked.

Jess' shock and fear gave way to anger.

"How am I supposed to know?" she said, throwing up her hands.

"All I know is some soulless blue-eyed jerk and a bunch of hooded figures grabbed me, rendered me unconscious, and stuck me in here. Playing evil music and evil holograms from ever slasher movie ever made. Now who are you?!"

Calm down, Jess, she thought to herself. *You're getting hysterical.*

The stranger looked at the mirror.

"Nice job, Stone," he said, smiling.

"I do my best," Stone said from the speaker.

Jess looked at the stranger.

"Who are you?"

The stranger laughed.

"You can call me...Lucifer."

"Satan!" Jess cried.

Lucifer chuckled.

"Yes, I guess that is one of the other titles I've been given."

Unable to stand any longer, Jess sat on the cot.

This can't be happening, she thought.

"So, the Devil wears Armani, huh?"

Lucifer looked at his clothes.

"It's comfortable, and I look good in it."

"I pictured you a little different."

"And how is that? Horns, tail, and a pitchfork?" he asked with a chuckle.

"I thought you would be better looking."

Come off it Jess, he is hot!

Lucifer frowned.

I'd rather have Tim, thank you very much.

"If I was in my full glory, you wouldn't be able to stand to look at me."

"I can't stand to look at you now."

Bold, girl!

Anger flared in his eyes. Then he laughed again.

Turning back to the mirror he said, "She's a real piece of work, isn't she?"

"Yes, sir," Stone said. "I find her feign bravery somewhat... charming."

"Gee, thanks," Jess said laying back on the cot, covering her left arm over her eyes.

"You are a bold one, aren't you?" Lucifer replied.

"What did you expect?" Jess asked.

"Aren't you scared?"

Jess sat back up.

Try terrified!

"Scared? Right now, I'm angry and freaking out! I've been kidnapped for some untold reason and I'm having a conversation with the Devil himself! The only comfort I get from this fact is you can't kill me!"

"Who says I can't kill you?" Lucifer asked.

Jess took a breath.

Crap! Have I said too much?

Hadn't one of her captures said they couldn't kill her?

"I-I was told that by one of your people."

"Oh, really?" Lucifer asked. "What makes you think that that was the truth?"

Jess thought.

Lord, help me, she prayed.

"Because, if you were allowed to kill me, I'd be dead."

Lucifer laughed.

"Why would I kill you before I tell you what I want?"

"What do you want? Why am I here?"

Lucifer grabbed an apple from his left pocket and a knife from his other pocket.

He began cutting the apple.

"Do you want a piece?" he asked Jess.

Jess looked at the apple, then back at him.

Lucifer laughed again. "It's the apple, isn't it? So very stereotypical of Satan offering an apple to someone, right? Okay, I'm not allowed to kill you. Happy now? Come on, do you want a bite or not? The apple is perfectly fine. You're getting Snow White and The Fall mixed up."

Jess' stomach growled.

"What do you mean?" Jess asked, trying to ignore her stomach.

"Well," Lucifer said, taking a cut piece of the apple and eating it, "You see, Snow White was given a poison apple that put her to sleep. In the story of The Fall, the identity of the fruit from the tree of knowledge of good and evil is never actually mentioned."

"What's your point?" Jess asked.

"My point is," Lucifer said, taking a bite of another slice, "that even though the apple is the stereotype, the real fruit has been lost to history."

Right! Jess thought.

She had no idea how long she had been held captive, or when she might eat again.

"How long have I been here?" she asked.

"Hmm. A while, I suppose. Take a piece."

Reluctantly, Jess accepted it and ate the bite he gave her.

Jess' eyes widened.

"Mmm..."

"Not bad, I take it?"

The best ever! She thought.

"It... wasn't bad," she agreed.

"Come on; be honest. The best apple you ever tasted, right?"

"Honesty? Coming from you? Yeah, right."

Lucifer frowned.

"Why am I here?" Jess asked. "What do you want?"

"What do I want?" Lucifer asked. "I want you to learn the truth."

Jess laughed.

"The truth? The truth about what?"

Lucifer looked into Jess' eyes.

"The truth about me and the One who sits on the Throne."

Jess looked back at him.

Here we go...

"You want to tell me your interpretation of what went on in Heaven that led to you being cast out? Are you mental?"

"He has deceived you."

"God has deceived me? He's not the one who kidnapped me, is He?"

"He's filled that Book with lies! He is not all-powerful, the Throne is!"

Jess just looked at him.

The Throne? Really? That's your play?

"Yes! It's the Throne that really has the power! I figured it out, you see! It's the Throne that created all of us angelic beings, He was created before me! We were all supposed to be able to sit on that Throne, but He wouldn't share! When I went to tell Him it was my turn, He had the other angels to block me. Me and the others! We knew that if we could get Him off the Throne, He wouldn't hold the power. I still have excess to Heaven because the Throne lets me. The Throne doesn't play favorites, I know that. It wants me to have a chance on it. But it will not remove the One that sits on it, because it wants us to work it out ourselves."

"That's original," Jess said. "I've never heard that one before."

I can't believe this...

"That's because He doesn't want you to know the truth about what happened!"

"It's true," Stone's voice said. "I was with him when he went to confront the One on the Throne."

I didn't ask you.

"And why are you telling me this?" Jess asked out loud.

"Because I want you to know what a fake that God of yours is! Renounce him and join me! Help me take back what should be shared with every being of the Throne!"

"Renounce my God? Are you nuts?"

Of course he is, Jess thought. *But he's also very convincing to some.*

"Yeah, I guess you are!" she said. "God has done great things for me in my life!"

"But where is He now?" Lucifer asked.

Jess stood and walked to the window, seemingly ignoring the question.

He is with me, even to the end.

"And has He told you where your father is?"

Jess turned to face Lucifer.

"My father? He left my mom and me years ago."

"But do you know why he left? Do you know where he is? I do! Join me, and I can arrange a meeting with him."

Liar!

Jess put her hands in her back pocket.

She felt something in one pocket.

What's that? she wondered.

She pulled it out of her pocket.

And gasped.

The new Bible.

The one Jeff had tossed to her.

Lucifer looked at her and put away his knife.

"What is that? What do you have there?"

Jess ignored him and turned it on.

Lucifer walked over to her.

"What is that? Give it to me. Now!"

Lucifer tried to grab it...

...And was jolted and pushed away by an unseen force.

Lucifer dropped the apple and growled.

Jess looked at Lucifer.

This is where my God is now, she thought.

"It's a Bible, Satan."

"So it would seem," Lucifer said, as he rubbed his hand from the unexpected jolt he received.

"Give it to me," he said.

"Are you looking for another shock?"

"Silly girl," Lucifer said, waving his hand.

"That...gadget holds no power. It would seem I am not to take it by force."

Jess smiled.

You've no power over me, fool.

"You...you can't touch me."

Lucifer picked up the apple and walked over to where Jess was standing.

"No. At the moment, I am just not able to harm you."

He put his hand on her shoulder.

Jess froze.

Oh, crap! Oh, crap! Oh, crap!

"But that doesn't mean I can't touch you," Lucifer said as he caressed her cheek with his finger.

Ugh!

He took a bite of the apple.

"Understand?"

"Get away from me," she said through clenched teeth.

Lucifer chuckled.

"In the name of Jesus, get away from me!"

Behind the mirror, the two demons flinched.

Lucifer was pushed back four feet, dropping the apple, again.

He growled.

Jess gasped.

Jesus, be with me!

Lucifer looked up at the ceiling.

"We had a deal! As long as I didn't harm her, I could do what I wanted!"

Jess took a couple of steps back.

Lucifer looked at Jess again and smiled.

"Now, where were we? Ah, yes. That gadget of yours. I guess I can let you have it for a while."

"You can't exactly take it away from me."

Lucifer's eyes glowed red.

Easy, girl.

"Don't try me, Jessica. I can make your life a living hell! Do you understand?" He asked as he picked up the apple for the second time.

Jess nodded.

"Good!"

Lucifer looked at his watch.

"Oh, my, look at the time! Your friends should be coming any minute now."

"My friends?" Jess asked, her heart quickening.

Tim!

"Yes, coming to rescue the poor damsel in distress," he said, mockingly.

"Of course, I could release you. Save them the trouble of trying to find you. All you would have to do is join me."

"I will never join you!" Jess said.

"Hmm. You might want to change your mind. There is so much more I can do to them than I can do to you."

"What are you talking about?"

"Well," Lucifer said, scratching his beard,

"I wasn't given as many...restrictions on them as I was with you. I think it will be...pleasant for me."

"Liar!"

Lucifer chuckled.

"Stop chuckling like a mad scientist from one of those lame Sci-fi movies!"

"Oh, but don't you know? This is like a Sci-fi movie! We have monsters, mayhem, a variety of weapons, and much, much more! We even set up a link to the internet! All around the Earth, my followers are receiving e-mails with a link to this world! They can make their Avatars anything! Some will guard this fortress; others will be causing as much havoc as they can to your friends. You can have your friends avoid all this if you do one little simple thing: Renounce your God. Renounce Him and follow me."

"I hate you!"

Lucifer laughed again.

"I think you are almost ready. Doesn't that gadget of yours say you are to love everyone? Hmm?"

Jess ran a hand through her hair.

This can't be happening!

"It doesn't say I have to love you!"

"It doesn't? Does it say you have the right to hate me?"

"It says to hate sin. You are sin!"

"Am I? Where does it say I am sin? Doesn't it say, "He who knew no sin became sin?' Wasn't that Jesus, the One you follow, that became sin? So, aren't you supposed to hate Him?"

Tears began flowing from Jess' eyes.

She dropped to the floor and cried.

Lord, help me!

"You cannot blame me for the errors that are in that Book of yours. Soon you will learn that what I have told you is the truth. But, when you figure that out, it might be too late for your friends."

Lucifer walked up to Jess, hunched down, and raised her head with his finger.

"I am not the bad guy here. I have been thrown into a bad situation, and I'm trying to get out of it. I have been for some time now. I believe, with your help, you could convince your friends that I'm the good guy, and you could all help me."

Jess didn't say anything.

"I'll let you think it over."

Raising, Lucifer walked over to the window, looked at the apple in his hand, then tossed it outside.

He reached back in his pocket, pulled out another apple, and threw it on Jess' cot.

"In case you get hungry," he said.

Jess just stared at the apple on her cot but said nothing.

"By the way, the offer still stands about your father. Think it over. Get back to me."

Lucifer went through the window, changed back into a dragon, and flew away.

Jess wiped her tears away and checked her Bible for the reference of Jesus becoming sin.

Where is it? She thought as she typed in keywords.

"Here it is," she said out loud. "2 Corinthians 5:21 'For He hath made Him to be sin for us, Who knew no sin; that we might be made the righteousness of God in Him.'"

Jess sighed.

"Lord," she began to pray, "I believe Your word over Satan's lies. I know Jesus spent three days dead. I also believe He rose on the third day, as Your Word says. I know He became sin to cleanse me and whoever else would ask Him for forgiveness from our sins. As it says in Revelation, He is the Spotless Lamb who was slain. I believe Jesus no longer has those black and nasty sins on Himself anymore, that they are thrown away. Never to be remembered by the Father, The Son, or the Holy Ghost ever again. Thank you, Lord, for loving me, for protecting me, even in this evil place. If my friends are really coming -- no, coming or not-- I pray for their protection. Forgive me for any doubt that comes to my mind. I pray You would give me strength for whatever else is about to come. In Your Son's Holy name. Amen."

"Awe, how sweet," came a new woman's voice from the speaker. "Too bad He didn't hear you."

Jess stood, wiped more tears away, walked over to the mirror, and asked, "And you might be...whom?"

"You can call me Deli."

Jess laughed.

"'Deli', huh? I thought you demons, Satanists, or whatever you are, went by evil and creepy names. 'Deli' is kinda...pathetic."

"Don't try me, girl. Have you ever gone toe-to-toe with a demon before?"

"I just faced Satan himself! I don't care how ugly and strong you are, you can't do anything to me that God wouldn't allow."

"Whoo! Brave words coming from a helpless child who was just crying her eyes out a minute ago. I don't care if there are some rules we have to play by, you don't want to mess with me."

Jess shut her mouth before she said something she might regret.

Quit while you're ahead, Jess!

"God, be with me," she prayed again.

"Do not fear, child," a voice spoke from behind her.

Jess turned around.

In front of her, surrounded by light and wearing a white robe, an angel stood.

"Be of good cheer. The Almighty has heard your prayers. You are not alone."

Jess stood there.

"M-my friends? Are they-?"

"They are coming, being led by Michael himself."

"Michael? The Archangel?"

"The very same," he said.

"And you? What is your name?"

"You may call me—"

"Elonzo!" Deli cried.

Jess turned around in time to see a beautiful, blue-skinned woman flying out of the mirror and attacking the messenger angel.

Deli collided with the angel she had called Elonzo by name, making them both fly out the window.

"No!" Jess said running to the window.

She saw the two in the air, falling, fighting hand to hand.

"Well, that was amusing," Stone said from the speaker.

Jess looked back at the mirror.

"How did she...?"

"Demons aren't bound by the same restrictions you humans are when it comes to things solid," Stone said.

"Oh," Jess said, returning her gaze back to the fight outside.

"This is unreal," she muttered.

"Infidelity?" Elonzo said as he was falling.

"Shut up!" Deli said, grabbing his collared robe and punching him in the face.

"You will pay for ruining my beloved city!"

Elonzo used his legs to push Deli back.

Finally, they both landed on the ground, Elonzo on his back and Deli on her feet. Elonzo got up.

"It's been a long time, Infidelity," he said, wiping blood from his lip with the sleeve of his robe.

"Not long enough, you worm!" She said, drawing her bow staff.

"I don't want to fight you. I just came to deliver a message."

Deli laughed.

"Elonzo, 'Ready for battle,' ha! More like 'coward in a fight!'"

"Sodom and Gomorrah was a long time ago," Elonzo said.

"Sodom? Gomorrah? I don't care about Sodom or Gomorrah! Zeboim was what was mine! And you and your God had no business taking it away from me!"

"They were covered in filth! The abominations were a stench in the nostrils of the Almighty!"

"Stench? You reek worse than my city ever did!" she said, swinging her bow at Elonzo's head.

"You never even had the decency to step foot there!"

"I didn't have to!" Elonzo said, dodging her blows.

"Like here, now, I was just sent to deliver a message!"

Deli wasn't listening anymore. Caught up in her own anger, she blindly swung anywhere.

"Fine," Elonzo said, a bow staff appearing in his own hand. "If that's what you want."

Elonzo blocked an attack aimed at his ribs, shoved the staff into the ground, and used the momentum to lift his body in the air, kicking her in the face. Deli stumbled back, wiping the blood from her mouth with her hand.

Elonzo stood there.

"If that is all," he said, "I'll be going now."

"No!" Deli screamed, once again swinging her staff, connecting only with Elonzo's staff.

"I am not done with you!" she yelled. "I will have justice for my city!"

She swung high.

He ducked, swinging his staff low, pulling her legs out from under her.

Deli gasped as she hit the ground.

Elonzo stood over her, sword now in hand, ready to strike.

"Give me one good reason why I shouldn't send you to the Pit right now."

Deli looked around for something, anything that she might use to distract him.

She felt something by her thigh. She moved her hand there.

The apple! Deli thought. *Thank you, Lucifer!*

"Well?" Elonzo said.

"No thanks. I've got better things to do."

As she said that, she threw the apple at his head.

It distracted him long enough for her to get up and run back into

Lucifer's fortress.

"This isn't over, Elonzo!" Deli screamed just before she vanished into the building.

Elonzo put his sword away.

"No, it isn't," he said, just before he disappeared.

CHAPTER TEN

The dragon flew.

"I almost have her. Soon she will be mine!"

Lucifer laughed.

"It's almost too easy! She hates me, that's good!"

"A good starting point. A good-- what?!"

Something landed on the dragon's neck.

"What? Who's there?" Lucifer demanded, doing a mid-air roll, in a vain attempt to see who was on top of him.

"Announce yourself!"

"Over a billion different ideas and all you could come up with was three red suns and a red atmospheric planet?" the newcomer said.

"I like red. It's the color of blood, sue me. What do you want, Avdeel?"

"The Almighty wants a word with you," Avdeel said.

"Ooh! He has requested my presence. So, what? He can't get off the Throne and come to me?"

"That is not how it works, Satan."

"Bite me!" The Dragon roared.

Avdeel sighed.

"Look, one way or another, you are going to talk with the Almighty, be it by you walking in on your own, or me dragging you. Your choice."

Lucifer laughed.

"You? I am more powerful than you could ever dream! What makes you think you could drag me in *there*?"

"Well, I guess you asked for it," Avdeel said.

Before the dragon knew what was happening, Avdeel had him bound by chains.

"What!" Lucifer yelled.

In that very instant, Lucifer was transformed back into his tuxedo human-wearing form. Avdeel, right beside him, in the presence of the Almighty God.

Lucifer broke free of his bonds and looked at Avdeel.

"Don't you ever do that again, you hear me!?"

"Silence!" the voice of God rang out.

Lucifer fixed his tuxedo.

"Satan! You did not tell Me of your other recruits in this matter. The internet link and the avatars."

"Oh, no," Lucifer said, mockingly hitting his head as if he had forgotten something important.

"How terribly thoughtless of me! You're the One who claims to be all-knowing! Do I have to spell everything out for you?"

"Mind your tongue, Dragon!" Avdeel said.

"Shut up, Boy Scout!"

"Enough!" God said.

"You never told me how many of Jessica's friends would be trying to help her. Why should I tell You everything?" Lucifer demanded.

"Hear this, Satan! Not only have you opened a link for your followers to join in on your evil act, but you have also opened it for more of My children, as well."

"What!" Lucifer screamed.

"You can't do this! That link belongs to me, and me alone!"

"Nothing is completely yours, Satan!"

Lucifer seethed.

"One of these days," he said. "One of these days I will gather enough forces, and I will rip You off that Throne You think is Yours!"

Lucifer turned to walk away.

"Satan!" Avdeel said.

Lucifer eyed Avdeel.

"There is coming a day when you will be bound by chains again. When that happens, you will have a much harder time breaking them. I just hope that if I'm not the one to chain you, I will be there in the front row, watching."

Lucifer glared at Avdeel, as he left Heaven...

...And stepped into the control room.

"Lucifer, my lord," Stone said.

"What happened after I left?" Lucifer asked, still upset.

"Well, sir... After you left, Miss White said a prayer, and ended up in a verbal match with Deli."

Lucifer smiled.

"Infidelity's here? I thought I felt her charm. Where is she now?"

"Well, Elonzo showed up, and Deli attacked him. They both fall out of Miss White's window, fighting."

"Is that why Jessica is looking out the window like that?" Lucifer asked.

"It is, sir," Stone replied.

Lucifer laughed.

"Back to business. The internet link is up and running, yes?"

"Yes, sir, as you requested," Stone said.

"Good! Have someone keep an eye on it. I have been told that His followers have access to the link, as well."

Stone looked at Lucifer and asked, "How?"

"I don't know," Lucifer replied.

Lucifer looked at Jess through the mirror and asked, "Stone, did you get the information you wanted on Miss Jessica?"

"I did, sir. I have all the information right here," he said, holding up a small device.

"Well, then, for just a few minutes, send some Shadows to haunt

Miss Jessica, then tell her what you found out about her past. I'll be back."

Stone smiled and said, "If I may ask, sir, what will you be doing?"

"Oh, just flying around like I was, before I was so rudely interrupted," Lucifer said, as he vanished.

Stone smiled.

"Do you ever wonder what goes 'bump' in the night, Miss White?" he asked with a laugh.

Stone pressed the intercom.

"Control room Two to control room One, are you there?" Stone asked.

"Control room One to control room Two..." Lloyd said.

"We are here," Aaron finished.

"Good," Stone said. "I need someone to monitor the internet link. I have been informed that we will be getting uninvited guests."

"We can do that," Lloyd said.

"No problem," Aaron added.

"Good," Stone replied.

Trisha walked over and pressed the intercom button.

"Stone? This place is amazing! It's like it's from another world."

"You have no idea how right you are," Stone responded.

"Just so you know, your people are allowed outside."

"Isn't it hot out there? I noticed the three suns."

"It is not hot out there. The temperature out there is in the mid 70's. And before you ask, the monsters outside will not harm you, either. The crystal necklace of yours makes them obedient to you."

Trisha fingered her necklace.

"By the way, I would like you and Kim to come back here as soon as you can."

Trisha looked back at Kim.

She was using one of the many computers in the room.

Trisha pressed the intercom button again.

"We are on our way," she said.

"Good."

"Aaron, Lloyd," Trisha said.

"Tell everyone what Stone said about outside."

"Very well," the twins said

"Kim," Trisha called.

Kim looked up from the computer.

"Stone wants us with him, now."

Kim got up and followed Trisha.

As they walked, Trisha said, "This place is so cool! Aren't you glad you tagged along today?"

Kim laughed and said, "I was just about to ask you if you were glad you brought me to tag along."

Trisha laughed and put an arm around her little sister.

"You know, I thought about coming without you. Just thought about telling you to stay."

"I'm glad you brought me. I know at first, I was a little bit freaked out about all this. But now, I kinda like it. Thanks."

"When did you get so good with a computer?"

Kim smiled sadly.

"I had a lot of time when you ignored me."

Trisha stopped.

"I'm sorry for ignoring you like that. It's just with mom and dad...well, I just didn't think you were ready to do the things I've been doing."

Trisha looked straight at Kim.

"If you ever feel uncomfortable with doing the things I do, just let me know. I won't make you do anything you don't want to do. Got it?"

"Got it," Kim said.

"Come here," Trisha said, pulling her sister in for a hug.

"I love you, Kim," Trisha said.

"I love you, too," Kim replied.

"Come on. We better go see what Stone wants from us."

As they resumed walking, Kim said, "I think Aaron is pretty cute."

Trisha laughed.

"Aaron's cute? You don't think Lloyd's cute, too? They are Identical twins! They finish each other's sentences, for Pete's sake! I can only tell them apart because Aaron wears green most of the time and Lloyd wears blue."

"I can tell the difference," Kim replied.

Trisha laughed and said, "I think you've hung out with us way too long. I'm just glad one of us can."

"Who do you think is cute?" Kim asked while they continued to walk.

"That, dear sister, will have to wait for another time," Trisha said with a wink.

Trisha and Kim giggled.

"Here we are," Trisha said, entering the control room.

"Ah, the Conner sisters, back at last."

"Could you please just call me Trisha?"

"As you wish, Miss Conner. Trisha."

Trisha smiled.

"That's better."

Trisha looked around the room.

"Where did Deli go?" she asked.

"She bumped into an old friend. I'm sure she'll be back soon, though."

"Oh, Okay."

Trisha looked through the mirror and saw a bunch of shadows.

"What are those?" She asked, pointing into Jess' room.

"They are called Shadows," Stone said.

Bump! Hello, Jessica. We see you.

Jess turned her attention away from the window.

Bump! Bump!

She didn't hear any audible voices.

Bump! We know who you are.

A shadow.

Jess turned but didn't see anything.

Bump! We are right here!

More shadows.

114

Jess stood still.

She saw the shadows moving.

"What are you?" she asked, panicked.

We are Shadows. We are what goes bump in the night!

The Shadows continued to move all over the room.

Bump!

Jess turned around, watching the Shadows move around.

"What do you want?" she asked.

Bump! Bump! You!

"Get away from me!" Jess screamed.

No! Bump! We want you! Join us!

Jess felt defeated.

Bump!

She felt hopeless.

Bump!

"Stop it!"

Bump!

Jess looked down at her own shadow.

Bump! Bump!

A Shadow passed her shadow, and a feeling of fear came over her.

Bump! Jessica! We are here and we want you!

They passed her shadow again, and she felt tense.

They're attacking my shadow! Jess thought.

Bump!

"Get away from me!" she said again. "Stop it! Get away!"

Bump! Join us!

"Never!" Jess said. "Oh, God, help me!"

The Shadows gasped and stopped.

Bump! Never say that Name again! Bump!

They attacked her shadow again.

Just like with Satan, Jess thought.

They can't stand against the power of the name of God!

Bump! Join us! Help us!

"No! In the Name of Jesus, get away from me!"

Just like before, Stone flinched.

This time, Kim did as well.

Trisha didn't notice.

"I think I'll put her on mute for a while," Stone said.

Kim nodded.

The Shadows screamed and stopped.

Brat! It won't be that easy! Bump!

"Oh, yeah?" Jess said.

Brat! Shut up, fool! Join us! Bump!

"Jesus loves me," Jess started to sing.

Brat! Shut up!

They continued talking, but they didn't come near her.

"This I know, for the Bible tells me so," Jess continued.

Bump! Brat! Shut up!

"Little ones to him belong..."

Shut up! Shut up! Bump!

"They are weak, but He is strong!"

Bump! Quiet! Bump!

"Yes, Jesus loves me!" Jess continued to sing.

Bump! Shut up!

"Yes, Jesus loves me!" Jess said, running to the small bathroom and shutting the door.

"Yes, Jesus loves me! For the Bible tells me so!"

Bump! Come out! Brat! Come out now!

The Shadows continued to scream and shout, but they could not get her.

Bump! Come out!

CHAPTER ELEVEN

The first thing they saw was red.

Lots and lots of red.

"Where are we, Mars or something?" Plate asked.

"Plate!" Ashley exclaimed.

"What?"

"Why would we be on Mars?"

"That's what I would like to know."

"Enough," Michael interrupted.

"No, we are not on Mars."

"Then, where are we?" John asked.

"We are in the spiritual realm. A small part of it, anyway." Michael said.

"'A small part' of a Spiritual realm? What does that mean?" Plate asked.

"It means, young sir, that Satan has been allowed to use a small part of the spiritual world to do as he wants."

"Why is he allowed to use any of the spiritual world?" Tim asked.

"That is not for you or me to question," Michael responded.

"Only the Almighty needs to know."

"Sorry," Tim mumbled.

"It is quite alright. By asking, you learn more than you did before."

"Like, 'only the Lord knows', right?" Plate asked.

"Precisely," Michael said.

"Okay, then," John said. "Where do we go from here?"

Michael pointed.

"Do you see that building?"

The group acknowledged that they did.

"That is where they are keeping Jessica."

"Wow," Sarah said. "How far is it?"

"Hmm," Tim said. "According to my scans, it's 1.5 miles."

"A mile and a half?" Sarah exclaimed. "Michael, why is it so far?"

"Come on, Sarah," Plate said. "We walk that every day!"

"But still!" Sarah said.

Turning back to Michael, she asked, "Why is it so far?"

"On your journey, you must face obstacles. That is the reason for the distance."

"Great! What kind of obstacles?" Ashley asked.

"As I told you, human imagination will be used. You will soon find out."

"So, we couldn't have been dropped off into the complex, with guns a blazing, could we?" Tim asked.

"Tim!" Ashley yelled.

"What? I just wanna get in there, grab Jess, and get the heck out of there! Is that too much to ask for!"

"We just can't do it like that! This isn't one of your stupid video games, you know."

"This is real!"

"Enough!" Michael said. "Remember what I told you? You must work together on this. You must work as one, do you all understand?"

"Yes, sir," Tim said. "I just wish there was an easier way to get Jess out."

"We all do, Tim," John said. "And we will get her out. Together, right?"

"Right," Tim said.

"We are going to get her out together, right?" John said again, looking at his friends.

"Right!" They said in unison. Even Theron joined in the rally cry.

"I guess we better get going, then," Theron said.

The group advanced forward.

"I have to get all the chairs up, sweep the floor, and make sure everything is put up!"

Julie was talking a mile a minute.

"Angels, demons, and battle suits!"

"Julie, are you okay?" Jack asked.

"I've never experienced anything like this! I need to get back and finish closing up the shop and get home!"

"Do you want me to drive you over?" Jeff asked.

"No, no. I'll be fine," Julie said, wiping tears from her eyes.

"Julie, here's the keys to my car, take it back to the shop, make a note letting Toby know we won't be opening up tomorrow morning. Lock up and go home. Leave my car there. Can you do that?" Jack asked her.

Julie wiped more tears from her eyes.

"Yes. Yes, I think I can do that."

After Jack gave Julie his keys, she walked over to where Liz was sitting, bent down, and gave her a hug.

"I'm sorry I can't stay," she whispered in Liz's ear.

Liz looked at Julie and said, "Pray for Jessica."

Julie nodded and made her way to the exit. Before she left, she turned around one more time.

"Sorry," she said.

Then she was gone.

Jeff looked at the door where Julie had just been.

"Will she be okay?" he asked, worry in his voice.

"I don't know if any of us will be okay," Jack said, looking at Liz.

"We'll have to wait for the dust to settle when this is all over."

Jeff nodded.

Pastor Stevens walked over to Liz and put his hand on her shoulder. "Liz?"

"Hmm?"

"Can I get you anything to drink? Maybe some water, coffee, or a soda?"

"Water would be great, thanks."

"One water, coming up," Pastor Stevens said.

As Pastor Stevens left, Jack and Jeff came over with a couple of chairs between them.

"Do you mind if we sit with you?" Jack asked.

"That would be fine," Liz said.

"I know it's a stupid question, but how are you holding up?"

Liz sighed.

"As well as can be expected, I suppose."

Jack grabbed her hand and squeezed it.

Liz squeezed back.

"We are here for you. You know that, don't you?"

"Yes, thank you, Jack."

Pastor Stevens came back with a bottle of water.

"Liz," he said, holding the bottle out to her.

"Thanks," Liz said, taking the bottle and holding it.

Pastor Stevens smiled and then walked over to talk with Bobby, who was using the computer.

"Bobby?"

Bobby looked up from the computer screen.

"Yes, Pastor?" Bobby asked.

"Bobby, I think it's time you went home. Maggie will take you home, so you don't have to call your father."

"Can't I stay for a few more minutes? Twenty minutes, please? Then I'll go home."

"I'll watch him for the twenty minutes then take him home, if that's alright with you, Pastor," Maggie said.

Pastor Stevens looked from Bobby to Maggie.

"Twenty minutes, no more. Then he has to go home."

"Thanks, Pastor," Bobby said.

"You're welcome," Pastor Stevens said, walking away.

"Jeff, can I talk with you, alone?" Pastor Stevens called.

Jeff looked over from where he was seated.

"Sure," he said, getting up.

He turned back to Liz and Jack and said, "I'll be right back."

As Jeff walked up to Pastor Stevens, he asked, "What's up?"

The Pastor gave a wearied sigh.

"I'm going to be in my office for a while. I feel like something's missing, and for some reason, I feel that maybe something is in my office somewhere. If anything else happens, come and tell me, okay?"

"Okay, Pastor."

Pastor Stevens shook his head.

"I don't like this. Keep praying."

"I still am," Jeff said.

"Good." Pastor Stevens said as he walked away.

Jeff walked back to Jack and Liz and noticed they were petting Bobby's dog.

"It's the strangest thing," Jack said.

"What is?" Jeff asked, taking his seat.

"This dog," he said. "In all my life, I have never had a dog like me, yet this one here is enjoying mine and Liz's company."

Jeff smiled.

"That's great, Jack."

Just then, the theme of "Mission Impossible" started playing.

Jack stood up and fumbled for his cell phone.

"That's me. Sorry, I got to take this."

Jack walked away and when he got out of earshot, he answered the cell phone.

"Hello?" Jack asked.

"Mr. Pippirelli?"

"Yes."

"Your password, please."

Jack sighed. He knew that the person on the other end had already done a voice print confirming it was who he said he was.

"Screwtape," Jack said.

"Excellent. How are you, Jack?"

"I've been better, to tell you the truth."

"Do tell."

"You didn't call me to ask how I was. What do you want?"

"It would seem that a few of your associates are in a bit of trouble, am I right?"

"What are you talking about?" Jack asked, annoyed.

"Your friends are on a mission of sorts."

"What do you know? How did this show up on your radar?" Jack asked.

"Our computer techs have stumbled across a website of...unusual origin."

"What do you mean 'Unusual origin?'" Jack asked.

"Well, in layman's terms, we know it's located in your area, we just can't find it."

"That helps," Jack said rubbing the bridge of his nose.

"What does that have to do with me?"

"Do you have internet capabilities?" the Stranger asked.

"Hang on."

"Sure."

"Maggie!" Jack called.

Maggie looked up.

"Does that thing have the internet?"

"I don't know. Let me check!" Maggie answered.

"I think the other computer does," Bobby said.

Maggie went to the other computer and checked for a connection.

"Yes, Jack," Maggie answered. "This one does."

"Yes," Jack said into the phone, walking over to Maggie.

"I have a computer. Now what do you want me to do?" Jack asked, sitting in the chair.

"What's going on Jack?" Maggie asked.

Jack shook his head to let her know it was not a good time to ask him anything. The voice on the other end gave Jack a web address.

"Okay, here we go."

"Very good," the voice said.

When the page loaded, Maggie gasped.

"Oh, my!" Jack said.

"I take it the page loaded," the voice said.

"You got that right," Jack replied.

"Then I will let you go now."

"No! Wait!"

The line disconnected.

"My goodness," Maggie said, as she stared at the computer screen.

"You got that right," Jack said.

Turning around, Jack called for Jeff.

"Jeff, I think you'll wanna see this!"

As Jess hid in the small bathroom, she examined her small Bible device a little closer. She found a song list in the device and a set of earphones in a small compartment. She decided to play the song "Jesus Love Me," having an earphone in one ear, leaving the other ear unoccupied, in case her kidnappers wanted to converse with her. She had noticed that the Shadows had stopped harassing her, for the time being. Jess let another song play.

"Jessica?"

Jess stopped the song.

"Oh, Jessica?"

She removed the earphones from her ear.

"It's okay, Jessica, I'm not going to ask you to come out of there; I know you can hear me."

Stone! What does he want now? Jess thought.

"You see, Jessica, I have come across some interesting information about you. I'm sure you'd like to hear it."

What is he talking about?

"You see, the information I'm talking about is stuff no one else knows. Stuff that your God claims to be forgiven and forgotten. You know, evil thoughts, actions, or hurtful words you might have used."

Jess opened the door and walked out.

"What are you talking about?" Jess demanded.

"Ah, I see that you are listening. By the way, I have you on mute, so I don't have to hear your moaning and groaning."

Jess stared at the mirror.

Stone laughed.

"You look rather annoyed, Miss White. I'm hoping for shame and embarrassment after I tell you what I've found on you."

"It wouldn't matter," Jess said. "Whatever it is, God has forgiven me!"

"There you go again, talking to me like I can hear you."

Stone laughed again.

He doesn't really think this is funny, he just wants to annoy me with that stupid laugh of his.

"Let's see," Stone continued on. "Ah, here is a nice one. It takes place a month after you first moved to Forsaken & Forgotten. You were all alone in your house. Do you remember that? Your mother was working later than usual, and you had decided to watch a horror movie."

Jess paled.

Oh, no. Not that one, please, Lord.

Stone laughed again.

"From the look on your face, you remember that, don't you?"

Not knowing what else to do, Jess nodded.

"Good," Stone said.

"Let's see...Your mother was working late, so you decided to stay up late and wait up for her, at least that is what you told her when she got home. Anyway, you were channel surfing and came across a horror movie on the 'After the kiddies have gone to bed hour.' You never watched a horror movie in your life, so you thought you would treat yourself to one. You were, after all a teenager in the house all by yourself, right?"

I remember, Jess thought. *I also vowed never to watch another horror movie in my life.*

"The movie centered on a small town with a psychotic killer who escaped from the mental ward in the hospital two towns over after killing everything in sight, from the goats, sheep, cows, horses, cats, and dogs to the innocent kids, men, and the barely dressed women. Nothing was spared. If it could be maimed, tortured, blown up, or violated in any way, it was done."

Stone laughed.

"I believe that movie went on to spawn 32 sequels, and they are filming one more even as we speak."

Jess' stomach turned.

"Anyway, after the movie had ended, your mother came home, and you told her that you stayed up waiting for her and that there wasn't anything on, so you decided to read a couple of your magazines until she got home. Then you both went to bed. Sometime after you fell asleep, you started dreaming that you were killing all sorts of animals and torturing the townspeople and enjoying it. You then woke up in a cold sweat, crying. You ended up waking your mother up and admitting to her what you had done."

Jess remembered that night, and what her mom had said.

"Jessica, honey," Liz had said, moving the hair from her daughter's face.

"I thought you knew better than to watch trash like that."

"I do, and I'm sorry. I'm so sorry, Mom" Jess had said, crying in her mother's arms.

Stone laughed.

"You then had to sleep in the same bed with your mother for a month before your nightmares would stop."

"I have been forgiven of all that, and of everything else you think you can use against me!"

Stone laughed.

"My, my, my. I seemed to have hit a nerve. Remember, you are on mute, my dear. Let's try for another, shall we?"

Jess fell to her knees and prayed.

Stone laughed.

"Begging will get you nowhere, my dear."

"Lord," Jess prayed, "I thank You for forgiving me of my sins and where I have failed You in my life."

"Let's see," Stone said.

"I pray, Father, that You would hamper the plans of Stone's continued effort to hurt me in this way. I know You have forgiven me for my past, but it hurts to have it shoved back into my face like this. Help me, please, Lord."

Stone laughed.

"Oh, Jessica, this is a good one, I'm sure you will enjoy hearing it as much as I am just reading it - what! Turn off the microphone! Turn it off!"

Jess couldn't help having a little chuckle over the shock in Stone's voice.

"Lord, whatever You did, thank You."

Stone laughed as he watched Jess fall to her knees.

"Begging will get you nowhere, my dear."

"I don't think she's begging; I think she's praying," Trisha said.

Stone didn't seem to hear her. He was reading something from his device.

Stone laughed again.

"Oh, Jessica, this is a good one," Stone said, menace in his eyes.

"I'm sure you will enjoy hearing it as much as I am reading it-- what!"

Just then the device began to spark and smolder.

"Turn off the microphone! Turn it off now!"

"The microphone is off, sir," Kim said.

Stone swore.

"What's wrong? What happened?" Trisha asked.

"This - this stupid contraption just literally blew up in my hand, that's what happened!"

"What?" Trisha said. "Are you okay?"

"I'm fine!" Stone barked, throwing the smoking device against the wall where it broke into pieces.

Stone then pushed the intercom. "Control room 2 to control room 1," Stone said.

"Control room 1 to control room 2, go ahead," a voice said.

Trisha looked at Kim and mouthed, *Aaron or Lloyd?*

Aaron, Kim answered back, smiling.

Trisha smiled back at her sister.

"Control room 1, send the skunkmare into Miss White's room, will you?"

"Yes, sir," Aaron said, "right away, sir."

When Stone was finished, Trisha asked, "What's a skunkmare?"

"You shall soon find out, my dear," Stone said. "You shall soon find out."

CHAPTER TWELVE

As Pastor Stevens walked into his office, he prayed, "Lord, what is in here, what do You want me to see?"

He received no answer.

Pastor Stevens walked over to his desk and sat down.

There he noticed all the unopened mail that had been collected during the week.

It's definitely been a busy week, Pastor Stevens thought.

"Lord," he prayed again, "What have we missed? What have I missed? Please, reveal whatever it is to me so I might know how to handle this situation."

He looked again at the pile of mail and picked it up.

Underneath the mail was a manila envelope. Pastor Stevens sat the other mail down and grabbed it.

"What's this and how long has it been here?" he said to himself.

He checked the postmark and calculated that he must have received it last Thursday or Friday.

"Must have been busier than I thought," he said, putting the envelope back down.

The envelope, open it.

Pastor Stevens sat straight up in his chair.

"Lord?" He asked.

No answer.

Pastor Stevens picked the envelope up and opened it.

He let the contents slide out of the envelope and onto his desk.

What fell out was a DVD case and a standard mailing envelope.

He first looked at the blank DVD case and then decided to open the other envelope first. Inside was a letter from a pastor friend of his:

Hey, Ron!

How is everything going with you? With this letter, I'm adding a DVD from our Wednesday night Bible study. Don't worry, I wasn't leading the lesson, so you don't have to listen to an old windbag like me.

Anyway, over the last few weeks, we have had a guest speaker lead the class studies on spiritual warfare, Satanism, Cults, and other avenues of Satan. I tell you, Ron, in all my years, I was still shocked to learn what was being taught to us. Satan is a great deceiver, and he is using anything he can to do so.

Ron, the Lord laid it on my heart to send you this DVD. I feel there is a storm brewing, and you are right in the middle. I don't know when the storm will hit, the Lord didn't reveal that to me, but I feel it will be soon. I am praying for you.

Your brother in the Faith,

Harold W. Marks.

Pastor Stevens laid the letter down.

"Oh, Harry," Pastor Stevens said, as he picked up the DVD case.

"I just wish I would have seen this sooner."

Jeff was sitting with Liz, petting Lex when Jack called him over.

"I'll be right back," he told Liz.

Liz nodded and continued to pet Lex.

Lord, be with her, Jeff prayed as he got up.

When he reached Jack, he asked, "What's up?"

"Take a look for yourself," Maggie said, giving Jeff room to see.

Jeff stared at the screen in shock.

On the screen was a picture of Jessica White in the upper left corner, and a story filling up the rest of the page.

Jeff read the screen:

Welcome, Servants of the Dark Master! The time has come to reduce the Kingdom of Light into rubble! The Dark Master has captured the daughter of his enemy, the Shining King! In response, the Shining King has sent some of his trusted warriors to try and bring His daughter back. Join us as we crush those who get in our way! Help guard our fortress while the Dark Master extracts the information needed to bring down the Kingdom of Light! Choose any weapon from a vast arsenal! Choose any form you wish to fight as. From giants or trolls, humans or animals!

"You have got to be kidding me," Jeff said, looking up from the screen.

"There's more," Jack said. "Take a look."

Jack scrolled down to give Jeff a better look:

Among the warriors the Shining King has sent, there are five special warriors. Destroy them, and the army He has sent will crumble under our feet!

Under that proclamation were five pictures. A picture of John, Plate, Tim, Sarah, and Ashley, each in their battle armor. Under the pictures, was a link that said:

CLICK HERE TO PLAY!

"I don't believe this!" Jeff said, running a hand through his hair. "They are making a game of this!"

He then looked at Jack and asked, "How did you find this?"

Jack looked rather uncomfortable.

"Come on, Jack! This is Jessica and the kids we're talking about here!"

"Okay, I'll tell you. But I think we need to let Liz see this first."

Jeff looked over at Liz and back to Jack.

"Are you crazy? She already has enough to deal with! She's barely hanging on as it is!"

Jack sighed.

"It's like you just said, Jeff. This is Jessica we are talking about."

"I agree with Jack," Maggie said. "She needs to know."

Jeff looked at Jack, then Maggie.

"Fine! I'll bring her over, but I still don't like this."

This is crazy! Jeff thought as he walked over to get Liz.

Pure insanity! They kidnap Jess, then they make a game of it!

"Liz?" Jeff said once he reached her side.

"Hmm?" she responded.

Oh, Lord, please be with her! Jeff prayed.

"There is something we think you need to see. It's over at the computer."

"Okay," she said.

"You want me to help you up?" Jeff asked, extending his hand.

Liz took his hand and held onto him as they walked.

She is in total and complete shock; is this really even her?

When they got to the computer, Jack gave up his seat so Liz could sit down.

"Liz," Jack said. "We thought it was very important that you see this."

Liz nodded.

Jack turned the chair so Liz could read the screen.

Liz gasped.

"Oh, my baby!" Liz said, then she fainted.

"Liz?" Jeff said. "Liz, can you hear me?"

Angered, Jeff looked at Jack and yelled, "See what you did? I told you she had already had enough, but you insisted that we show it to her anyway!"

"She had the right to know! Jessica is her daughter, for crying out loud!"

"Would you two knock it off?" Maggie said, checking Liz's pulse.

"Liz's breathing and heart rate is normal. I think it might do her some good to rest right now. Bobby, could you go to my office? Behind my door is a cot. Could you get it for me?"

"Yes, ma'am," Bobby said.

"So, she's okay?" Jeff asked, still fuming.

"Yes," Maggie answered.

"Good. I need some air," Jeff said as he headed outside.

Jack looked at Liz, then at Maggie.

"Are you sure she's okay?"

"Yes. Yes, I am."

Jack sighed.

"Good."

Bobby came back with the cot and set it up.

"Thanks, Bobby," Maggie said.

"But do you think you could set it up outside this room, by the wall?"

"Sure," Bobby said.

"Jack, do you think you can lift Liz and put her on the cot, or should we just roll the chair over there?"

"I got her, no sweat."

Jack picked Liz up and carried her to the cot.

Once Maggie and Jack made sure Liz was comfortable, they went back to the computer.

Bobby was sitting in the chair looking at the screen.

"Bobby, I think now would be a really good time for me to take you home," Maggie said.

Bobby looked up from the screen.

"I think I found something you might wanna take a look at," Bobby replied.

Maggie walked up to the computer and Bobby pointed to the screen.

"There," he said.

Maggie looked at the screen.

"What in the world?"

She then looked up at Jack.

"Jack, go find Jeff."

"I'm not sure he wants to see me right now."

"Jack, please."

"Okay," Jack said, heading outside.

As soon as Jeff walked outside and sat down, he started praying.

"Lord, I ask you to protect Liz. I have no idea what she is going through. But, Lord, I know You know. Give Liz the strength to get through this. I pray, Lord, for Jessica, That You would be with her at this hour. I pray for her protection, Lord. Keep her safe. Lord, I also pray for me. Forgive me for where I have failed You. Give me the strength to be the man You want me to be. Use me in the way You deem fit for me. I pray for Pastor Stevens, Lord. Make him an even better Pastor than he is now. I pray You would use him in a mighty way, Lord. For Maggie, Lord. Give her strength, Lord. Bless her. Give her the words to help those that have been in her situation, and those who haven't, Lord. Give her Your wisdom on how to handle the difficult things that will come her way. I pray for John, Tim, Plate, Sarah, and Ashley, Lord. Protect them from harm. I pray that they and Jessica would come out of this stronger than when they went in. I pray, Lord, you would protect Jack. He's a good man, Lord. I pray You would continue to use him in a mighty way, serving You. I pray, Lord, also for this town. Guide and protect this town. Use this town to glorify You. I pray this, Lord, in Your Son's name, the name of Jesus. Amen."

"Amen."

Jeff turned around and saw Jack standing there.

Jack cleared his throat.

"Sorry, I heard you praying, and I didn't want to disturb you."

Jeff stood and walked over to Jack.

"It's fine. Listen, I wanna apologize for blowing up at you. I was wrong, and I'm sorry."

Jack pulled him in for a hug.

"I'm sorry, too. This is a rough situation we're in. Tempers are flaring 'cause we're all scared."

Jack released Jeff from his embrace.

"Yeah, I guess so," Jeff said.

"Anyway," Jack said, changing the subject.

"Bobby found something else on the computer and Maggie wanted me to get you."

"Then let's go," Jeff said.

"My thoughts, exactly," Jack said, opening the door.

CHAPTER THIRTEEN

Screech!

Jess turned to face the window.

Screech!

"What in the world?" Jess asked out loud, as she walked over to the window.

Screech!

Jess looked out the window and noticed a strange, skeletal-looking creature flying.

The strange, flying creature was holding another strange creature.

Jess watched as the two creatures approached the window, quickly.

They're going to come in here! Jess thought.

She backed away from the window, heading for the bathroom.

The flying creature threw the other creature into the room and flew away.

Jess stood in shock.

The strange creature resembled a skunk, only its appearance was three or four times the size of a regular skunk and its body color was orange with a blue strip, contrary to a normal skunk's black and white look and it had reptilian-like skin.

Jess took a step back.

The creature snarled, revealing it had no teeth.

Why doesn't that make me feel any better? Jess thought.

Jess took a breath and tried to think.

Can I make it to the bathroom?

The creature took a step forward; Jess took another step back.

Jess looked around.

If I can get into the bathroom, I'll be fine. It can't go in there, right?

Jess slowly took a step to the side, in an attempt to get the creature circling.

The creature took the same sidestep, blocking the door to the bathroom.

There goes that idea. Jess thought.

Okay...Now what?

Jess looked around the room, hoping to find something to distract the thing.

She looked towards her cot and noticed the untouched apple, the one Lucifer had tossed onto her cot.

Jess took a step to her cot.

The creature did not move.

She took another step.

Still, nothing.

Finally, Jess made her way to the cot and grabbed the apple.

The creature tilted its head.

"Do you like apples?" Jess asked.

The creature remained unmoving.

What now?

Jess looked past the creature, out the window.

I wonder... Jess thought.

Could I trick this thing into jumping out the window for the apple?

This is crazy! Still, what else can I do, and what do I have to lose?

Taking a deep breath, Jess stepped away from the cot.

The creature made no move, only watching her with its eyes.

"Do you like apples?" Jess asked again.

Jess slowly sidestepped her way to the other side of the wall, hoping she might be able to get the monster to circle her for the second attempt to escape to the bathroom.

Here goes nothing, she thought.

The creature made no move to stop her.

What if it doesn't move? Jess thought in a panic.

What if it just stays in front of the door?

Oh, please let it move! Jess half thought, half prayed.

As Jess slowly made it to the window, the creature slowly turned itself so it could continue to watch her.

It's a start!

"Hey, there, buddy. Do you like this apple? Huh?"

The creature just looked at her.

I must be crazy, talking to this thing like that!

Jess looked behind her to make sure she was at the center of the window.

At least that part worked. Thank You, God!

Jess held out her hand that held the apple.

The creature snarled.

Without thinking, Jess pulled her hand back a bit too quickly.

The creature took a step back.

Jess sighed with relief.

No sudden movement, Jessica! That thing could have attacked you!

"Okay, then," Jess said to the creature. "No more sudden movements, okay?"

Again, the creature just looked at her.

"I'll take that as a 'yes,'" Jess said.

Jess held the apple up, holding it with two hands.

"Do you like apples? I've already had a piece today. It's good. Would you like it?"

The creature took one step forward.

"Is that a yes?" Jess asked.

The creature tilted its head again.

Please just be admiring the fruit.

Jess held the apple out a little bit farther from her body, but not as far as before.

The creature took another step forward.

Jess had to fight the urge to back up.

Any closer to the window, and you might fall out with it!

"That's a good boy. You do like apples, don't you?"

The creature took another step.

Jess' heart started pounding.

Don't panic! It just wants the apple!

"That's it! Yeah. It's a nice apple, isn't it?"

The creature took another step forward.

What am I doing? What am I supposed to do? Let it take the apple from my hand, then try and flip it out the window. Jess, what are you thinking!?

Before Jess could think another thought, the creature lunged at her. The creature pinned Jess to the floor, causing her to drop the apple out of her hands. Without thinking, Jess drew her legs up and under the creature and pushed with all her might. The creature hit the mirror, stunned.

Oh, no! Jess thought, stunned, *what just happened?*

Before Jess could think about doing anything, the creature shook its head and looked at Jess. It then turned around and lifted its tail.

"Oh, no," Jess said, having a good idea of what was to come next.

As she had guessed, the skunk-like monster sprayed the room. A red cloud engulfed the room, giving off the sweetest-smelling aroma Jess had ever smelt in her life.

Jess laughed.

"Well, I wasn't expecting that!"

Jess laughed some more.

The creature went up to Jess' leg and started panting like a dog.

"That was totally gross! It gives off a sweet smell, but still gross!"

As the cloud dissolved, Jess continued to laugh and started scratching the head of the creature.

Jess picked up the apple and she and the creature walked over to the cot.

"Is that your way of making friends, boy? Like sniffing a hand, or something?"

The creature just looked at her and continued to enjoy the petting it was getting.

"So, what are you doing here?" she asked, giving it the apple to eat.

The creature took the apple in its mouth and swallowed it whole.

"Wow, I thought only snakes and some other reptiles did that."

Jess looked at the creature.

"What are you, anyway? You look like a skunk, but you have the skin of a reptile."

The creature just looked at her.

Jess laughed again.

"Are you still trying to figure me...?"

Before Jess could say another word, she passed out on her cot.

The creature looked at her one more time.

Then it jumped out the window.

"Is that it?" Trisha asked, astonished.

"All it does is spray her, knock her out, then leave?"

"Not quite," Stone said.

"Well, then, what else is there?"

"That was not a normal skunk," Stone told her.

"So I noticed," Trisha shot back.

Stone ignored the comment.

"Unlike a regular skunk, when the skunkmare sprays, it doesn't release a foul odor. Instead, it releases the sweetest smell you will ever know."

"No thanks. I'd rather not be sprayed by anything," Trisha said.

"That's because the last time we went camping, Trisha got sprayed by one," Kim said. "Mom wouldn't let her back into camp until Dad went and got the supplies needed to get rid of the smell."

"Kim!" Trisha said.

"What? It's true!" Kim said, innocently.

Trisha gave her little sister a look.

Kim tried not to laugh.

"Back to the matter at hand," Stone said.

"When the skunkmare sprays, the victims will stay a lot longer because they enjoy the aroma of it. They then pass out and experience horrific nightmares."

This piqued Trisha's interest.

"Too bad we can't see their nightmares. That might be fun to watch."

"Actually, we can," Stone said.

"Really?" Trisha asked, surprised. "How?"

Stone opened a cabinet drawer and pulled out what looked to be goggles.

"These are how."

Before Trisha could ask anything else, Deli walked into the control room, looking a bit upset.

"What's the matter, Deli?" Stone asked. "Your friend couldn't stay long?"

Deli gave Stone a sharp look.

"Bite me, Stonewraith!" she retorted.

Stone chuckled.

"You look like you could use a pick-me-up. We just had a skunkmare invade Ms. White's room and spray her. Would you like to do the honors of placing the goggles on her so we can see her nightmares?"

Deli gave an evil grin.

"It would be my pleasure."

Deli grabbed the goggles from Stone and walked through the two-way mirror. Trisha gasped and looked at Stone.

"Demons aren't bound to the same rules you are, Miss Conner."

"Right, I knew that," Trisha lied.

Trisha turned around to watch Deli put the goggles on Jess.

Stone grinned.

Deli put the goggles on Jess and positioned her fully on the cot.

When she was done, she walked back through the two-way mirror.

"Well," Deli said, "that should do it."

"Excellent," Stone said, bringing up a program on one of the computers.

"Interesting," Stone said.

"What?" Trisha asked.

"A skunkmare's victim usually has a real-time nightmare. That would mean that the nightmare they have lasts for only however long they are out."

"Yeah, and?" Trisha asked.

"Ms. White seems to be having a lengthy nightmare. At this rate, should she be unconscious for an hour, she will have had a six-hour-long nightmare. That works out better than I could have hoped for."

Trisha turned to her sister and said, "I don't think you should see this. Maybe you should find something else to do."

"I'll be fine, Trisha. I can handle it."

"Okay, if you say so," Trisha said.

"We might end up watching this like a fast-forwarding DVD, right, Stone?" Deli asked.

"We just might, indeed," Stone said.

Maggie was still looking at the screen when she heard footsteps.

Jack and Jeff walked into the room.

"Everything okay between the two of you?" she asked.

"Yes, Maggie," Jack said.

"What did you find?" Jeff asked.

Maggie pointed to the screen as they got closer.

Jeff and Jack stared at the screen.

In the bottom right corner of the screen, there's an image of a demon trying to keep a door closed. The door opens, sending the demon flying. Inside the door, there is a cross with the inscription "Come unto me" where the arms of the cross connect. The demon comes back, and the image repeats itself.

"Maggie, can you click on that?" Jeff asked.

"Sure," Maggie said, grabbing the mouse and clicking on the cross.

A new screen popped up.

"Amazing," Jack said.

"You got that right," Maggie replies.

"I think I need to go get Pastor Stevens now," Jeff said.

"Good idea," Maggie told Jeff.

"Michael?" Ashley asked.

"Yes?" Michael replied.

"I've been meaning to ask, why are there three red suns here, and we aren't burning up?"

"The red suns are Satan's idea. They provide no temperature here."

"Oh, okay," Ashley said.

"I see something!" John said. "Over there. Look."

"Tim," Sarah asked, "What does your scans show?"

"Give me a second," Tim replied.

"You have got to be kidding me!" He said once he had finished his scans.

"What?" Sarah asked.

"It appears to be people...except they have energy bars above their heads. Like what you see in video games."

"Come on, really?" Plate asked.

"I ain't making this up, Plate."

John looked at Michael.

"Are those bad guys, Michael?"

"At this time, I have not been informed."

"That doesn't help much," Plate said.

Michael gave Plate a hard stare.

Plate cleared his throat and said, "Sorry."

He then looked at Tim.

"How far are we from them, Tim?"

"About...less than a half a mile. I say we go say hello," Tim said, making his claws come out and then retracting them.

"What do you guys think?"

"Let's go," John said.

CHAPTER FOURTEEN

Pastor Stevens had played the DVD and watched a small part of it before he shut it off and shook his head.

"I wish I would have seen this last week when it came."

Pastor Stevens folded his hands and bowed his head.

"Lord, I know that Your ways are not our ways, and Your timing is not that of our timing. I pray that this was Your will that I find it now and that I didn't mess Your plan up by finding it now. If I did, Lord, I pray You will forgive me, and that this day of trial will be used to Your glory anyway. Protect Jessica and her friends, Lord. Give them strength. For without You, they can do nothing. I pray this in Jesus' name, Amen."

Pastor Stevens raised his head and looked at the DVD case again.

He put it down and was about to reach for the letter once more when there was a knock on the door frame.

"Pastor?" Jeff said.

"Jeff, come in. What is it?"

"Is your computer online?" Jeff asked.

"Yes, it is," Pastor Stevens said.

"Good, type in this web address."

Pastor Stevens typed in the address Jeff had given him.

When the screen loaded, he stared at the screen in shock.

He looked up and asked, "How did you find this?"

"Jack found it, sir," Jeff said.

Pastor Stevens read the page, looked back at Jeff, and asked, "Did he say how he found it?"

"No, um, he didn't have time. Something else happened."

Pastor Stevens looked at Jeff.

"What?"

Jeff looked uncomfortable.

"Liz. Liz fainted when she saw that."

"She what?" Pastor Stevens asked, jumping out of his chair, rushing out the door, almost knocking Jeff down when he did so.

"She's fine," Jeff said, running after him.

"Maggie said her breathing and heart rate is normal, and that she's resting."

Pastor Stevens was moving so fast that he barely heard what Jeff was saying. When he finally reached the other building, he saw Liz lying on a cot.

Pastor Stevens walked over and bent down.

"Oh, Liz," he said.

"She's all right, Pastor," Jeff said, coming up behind him.

"All right?" Pastor Stevens asked. "How can she be all right with Jessica being kidnapped and it being broadcasted over the internet?"

"Pastor," Maggie said, walking over. "Her pulse is normal, and given what has happened, I think it's a good thing that she fainted when she did. Now her body can calm down."

Pastor Stevens shook his head and prayed, "Give her Your peace, Lord."

Pastor Stevens stood up.

"There is something else I wanted to show you," Jeff said

Pastor Stevens looked at Jeff. "Yes, what is it?"

"Well, we found something. It's a door with a cross behind it and a demon trying to keep the door closed.

"We clicked on it."

"And?" Pastor Stevens asked.

"Well, you'll have to see for yourself."

Jeff and Maggie lead Pastor Stevens to the computer.

Bobby got out of the chair to let Pastor Stevens sit down.

"I think it's time for you to be going, Bobby," Pastor Stevens said.

"It's late and there is too much stuff happening here. It would be best if you went home."

"No, Pastor, it wouldn't be," Bobby said.

"Excuse me?" Pastor Stevens said.

"Bobby," Maggie said. "I know you must find this fascinating, but you really need to get home,"

"You are right. I do need to leave, just not in the way you would think."

"Bobby, honey, what are you talking about?" Maggie asked.

Without answering, Bobby walked to the cot where Liz was sleeping.

"I will be back," Bobby said.

Before anyone could say another word, a bright light surrounded Bobby and Liz. The light got so bright, they had to turn their heads. Within seconds the brightness lightened, and they could see a light over Liz. Bobby was nowhere to be seen. Everyone stood dumbfounded.

"I guess I really shouldn't be surprised, right?" Pastor Stevens asked.

Jack looked at Maggie and Jeff, then said, "With the way things have been going today? No, I guess not."

"Um...anyway, Pastor," Jeff said. "You should really look at the computer screen."

Pastor Stevens directed his attention to the computer screen and read:

The Dark One has taken the Shining King's Daughter captive and has recruited many to help him in his evil plans. Now, the Shining King has asked if anyone is willing to help His five warriors bring His daughter home. Choose from a huge stockpile of weaponry, armor, and vehicles. Are you willing? Will you help the Shining King?

Pastor Stevens turned his chair around so that he could face the others.

"How did you find out about this, Jack?"

Jack looked uneasy.

"Let's just say I still have contacts in the military."

"You mean you got this link from someone in the military?" Jeff asked.

"I just said that, didn't I?"

"But why would they call you with this information?" Maggie asked.

"They know who I associate with. They saw the kids' picture and called to ask me if I knew anything about it."

"There's more, isn't there?" Jeff asked.

"It's classified."

"Jack, come on--"

"Jeff, listen to me," Jack said. "All I know is the people who called me, they have some of their own men in there right now trying to close down the program. Now I can only assume that means trying to get Jess outta there, too. What these people do, that's classified. What they are doing now, I think I can tell you."

Jeff sighed.

"So, what do we do?" Maggie asked.

"I think we should see what adventures await us," Pastor Stevens said, turning around and clicking a button on the computer.

"Liz? Liz, wake up."

"Hmm?"

Liz opened her eyes and saw an almost familiar face.

"Who are you?" she asked.

"Don't you recognize me? I'm Bobby."

"Bobby? How can that be? Bobby is just a boy. You, you're a grown man."

"In all actuality, I'm an angel. Here, let me help you up."

Bobby gave her his hand and helped her up. When she stood, she noticed she and Bobby were on a floating platform of some kind.

"Am I dreaming? Where are we?" Liz asked.

"You have been given a gift from the Almighty God. Your body is at the church resting, and you are having a vision of what is going on in the same realm as Jessica."

"A vision?" Liz asked. "You mean like John the Revelator?"

"I didn't work that case, but yes, something like that."

"Well, then, where is she? Where's Jessica?"

"Over there," Bobby said pointing to a large building.

For the first time, Liz noticed the red atmosphere, the creatures, and the building.

"Oh, my! What horrible-looking beasts!"

"Do not be alarmed. They cannot see nor harm us."

"That doesn't make me feel any better. What about the kids?"

"They have the protection of the Almighty."

Liz looked around.

"Where are the kids?"

"They are entering on the other side. Let us move so we have a better look, shall we?"

The platform moved slightly so the two could have a better view of their surroundings.

"Which room is Jessica in?" Liz asked.

Bobby pointed to the highest window and said, "That is where she is."

As Liz looked, she saw a blue and orange creature jump from the same window.

The creature fell a long fall and ran once it hit the ground.

"Oh, my! That thing was in the same room as Jessica! Is she alright?"

"Physically, yes. The creature knocked her out with its spray. Her dreams will torment her now."

"Oh, no! Please, Lord, no!" Liz prayed, falling to her knees.

Bobby put his hand on her shoulder.

"The Lord is with her," he said.

When they were within fifty yards, they noticed two different groups standing by a pay phone type box. One group looked to be military, with a variety of weapons; the other group was dressed in a variety of different media, from mythology and medieval times to futuristic-looking dresses.

"The one group seems to look a lot like the way we're dressed, don't you think?" Plate asked.

"A little bit," John said. "They haven't attacked us yet. I think that might be a good thing."

When they were just a short distance away, they stopped.

"I don't see the energy bars displayed above their heads," Ashley told Tim.

"Hmm, maybe I can only see it inside my suit."

"Could be," Ashley replied.

"Michael, Theron," Plate said, "Either one of you want to go talk with them and see if they are friend or foe?"

Michael and Theron looked at each other.

"That is something one of you must do," Theron said.

"Does that mean they are good guys. Other angels, I mean?" Plate asked.

"Check for yourself," Michael said.

"I'll go and see what I can find out," John said. "Theron, would you mind accompanying me just in case I need some backup?"

Theron smiled.

"That is something I can do."

John and Theron walked a short distance to meet up with the group of people.

When they were close enough, one person from each of the two groups walked over to John and Theron.

John studied the two people walking up to him. The first one was dressed like a typical military guy you would see in the movies or on the news; The other one was wearing all black armor, except for a gold helmet, with a golden cross in the center of his chest.

As the two approached closer, the military guy spoke first.

"Sir," he said with a salute.

Not knowing what else to do, John saluted back.

The military guy continued.

"Commander Tank, at your service! I am the team leader on this mission. We are here to assist you in taking down the fortress and shutting down its program."

Before John could say a word, the other one spoke.

"And I am J9M, part of the Elite Christian Hackers. E.C.H for short. We are also here to help bring the site down."

John just looked at the two as if they were nuts.

"What are the two of you talking about? I'm here to rescue a friend."

Tank answered first.

"We are a special faith-based unit. Usually, we are sent in to close down buildings that are practicing the occult. Things like human sacrifices, kidnappings, drugs, and other things. We also close down websites that deal in the occult."

J9M looked at Tank, then back at John.

"We also hack into occult websites, though we do it without authorization. We have never been caught, but given what's going on, I'd say it might happen soon."

J9M looked at Tank.

Tank laughed.

"I have already told him that we will not make it a point to find him and his buddies that are lurking around here. This time."

"Hackers?" John said in disbelief. "What are you talking about?"

"Allow me to explain," Theron said. "Shortly before we came through the door, Satan connected his realm to the internet, inviting his followers to join in and torment Jessica, and to hinder your efforts in rescuing her. The Almighty then decided to create a back door for other Christians to enter and aid in your efforts in getting Jessica."

"You mean this kidnapping scheme is real?" J9M asked.

"Very much so," Theron said.

"You mean to tell me that this is on the internet, for everyone to see?" John asked.

"Yes," Theron answered.

"So, Tank and J…I'm sorry, what was your name again?" John asked.

"J9M. It's one of my screen names."

"So I guessed."

Turning back to Theron, he asked, "So, does that mean Tank and J9M are just avatars being controlled from the outside?"

"Yes. The only real people here are you, your friends, and the people that took Jessica."

"And the other angels that are here, right?"

"Yes."

"You mean I'm gonna see real angels on here? Sweet!" J9M said.

Theron looked at J9M and said, "You will not remember what we angels look like when you leave this place."

"Well, that sucks," J9M replied.

A thought struck John.

"Hey, why haven't you guys moved, anyway? You have been in the same spot for a while now."

"We could not go any farther until you and your group arrived," Tank replied.

"That box there gave us our instructions, we couldn't advance if we wanted to. And I really wanted to," J9M added.

"Give us a couple of minutes. I got to go tell my friends what is going on."

Tank and J9M nodded and went back to their groups.

"I can't believe this!" John said to Theron.

"When did you find out about this being a website?"

"It was revealed to me just as we reached those two back there."

John shook his head.

"This is getting really stupid."

Theron didn't say anything.

When they reached the group, Ashley asked, "Well? What's going on?"

"They turned this whole thing into a website," John said.

"They did what now?" Sarah asked.

"They connected this realm to the internet somehow. The people over there are avatars. One group is a faith base military group, and the other is an illegal team of Christian hackers."

"Christian hackers?" Plate asked. "Sounds cool."

"Until we told them that this was real, they thought it was just another occult website. Or at least J9M did."

"J9M?" Tim asked.

"Yeah, it's the Christian hacker's screen name. The other guy, his name is Tank. Don't know if it's a screen name or not. Also, I asked them why they hadn't moved, and they said that the pay phone box gave them instructions, telling them not to move until we got there. There may also be a bunch of occult followers there ready to give us a hard time."

"This is not going to be easy, is it?" Tim asked.

"You didn't really think it would, did you, Tim?" Ashley asked.

"I was hoping," Tim replied.

"You guys ready to roll?" John asked.

Everyone looked at each other.

"Ready as we'll ever be," Tim said.

The group moved forward.

Tank and J9M walked back over to greet them.

"I forgot to ask," John said, "How many men do you have together?"

"Together, we have sixteen," Tank said. "There are ten of my men and six of J9M's men."

John did the math. "Great! Twenty-three altogether: Sixteen avatars, five humans, and two angels."

"And a partridge in a pear tree," Plate joked.

John groaned. "Not now, Plate."

"Sorry, couldn't resist."

John shook his head.

"Plus the other angels, they can all be in at any time," Michael added.

———

Tim walked over to the box to take a look.

"I've been trying to figure out what that thing means," someone said.

Tim turned around.

Staring back at him was a bull-faced male in a brown cloak.

Looks like a bull monk, Tim thought.

"Hi, I'm Jexx, part of the Elite Christian Hackers. Only one page is readable, and that says to wait for you guys. The rest is just gibberish."

Tim smiled underneath his mask.

"I'm Tim. It would seem that I am able to read the rest."

"That's good to know," Jexx replied.

Tim began reading.

"Hey, guys!" Tim said when he had finished reading.

"What is it?" John asked walking over.

"There is a message here for us," Tim told him.

"For us? What does it say?"

Tim cleared his throat and began to read.

"'John, Tim, Plate, Sarah, and Ashley, you all are about to do battle with Satan and his minions. Be strong and know that the Lord God Almighty is with you. He is with Jessica at this time as well. You must know that not everything you face can be defeated with weapons. Your faith is your greatest weapon, hold onto it. You will have the very angels from Heaven helping you when you need them. They are at your very call. Beware of Satan's tricks, he is a great deceiver. When you are ready, gather in a circle around this box and pray. When you are done, the box will be gone, and you can walk through the gate. Remember: The Lord is with you.'"

Plate looked around. "I don't see a gate."

"It won't show up until we have prayed," Tim said.

"Right, sorry. Who left the message?"

"God did, or He had an angel put it here, no question about that," John said.

"That was a direct message from The Almighty Himself," Michael answered.

Tim took a breath.

152

A message from God Himself! Tim thought. *I should be this excited when I read my Bible. He's always leaving direct messages in there.*

"Okay, guys, are we ready to do this?"

"Do you think the message included the avatars when it said to gather in a circle and pray?" Plate asked.

"Wouldn't hurt, they are believers also," John replied.

"I'll bring the rest of my group," J9M said.

Tank did likewise.

When they were all in a circle, John prayed.

"Our most Gracious Heavenly Father, we come to You asking for Your protection in the things we have to face. We thank You, Lord, for the help You have sent our way, with these here Christian hackers and this faith unit. We ask You, Lord, for the protection of Jess. Lord, we love her and want her to be safe. We ask for strength, Lord, to do what You would have us do. May what we do here glorify Your Name. We pray this in the Name of our Lord Jesus, Amen."

"Amen!" everyone repeated.

When they looked up, the box was gone, and there was a gate swinging open.

"I hope this is the last entrance we have to use before we can get inside the building," Tim said.

When the group walked through the gate, they stopped.

They saw flying beasts and all sorts of land creatures.

"How come we could see the building, but not all this?" Tim asked.

"Not sure, but there must have been a reason," John said. "Michael, do you know?"

"No," Michael replied.

"Whoa!" Tim said, jumping.

"You okay, Tim?" Plate asked, worried.

Tim put a hand on his helmet and said, "Hang on and give me a second."

After a moment, Tim laughed.

"What is it?" Sarah asked.

"A complete inventory of every creature here downloaded into my suit. It just popped up on my screen."

"Cool," Plate said.

"Yeah, I guess," Tim said, "If you're into information overload."

Turning to the avatars, Tim asked, "Did you guys get an inventory too?"

Each one said no.

"Hmm. I wonder what that's all about?"

"It is needful for you to know what you will be facing," Michael said.

"But not anyone else?" Tim asked.

Michael was silent.

Tim shook his head. "I don't like any of this."

"Let's keep moving," John said.

After walking twenty feet, Tim stopped.

A device came out of his arm and flew into the air.

"What was that?" Ashley asked, stopping as well.

"Speaker," Tim said. "My suit has been working on making a small music device. I finally got it working to play the songs I got from Jeff's song list. You ready to hear it?"

"Sure."

Tim hit the play button and a random song played.

"I'm in the Lord's army" began playing.

Tim laughed.

"Jeff went all out, didn't he?" Tim said

"What a way to announce ourselves, huh?" Ashley responded.

Tim let the song play.

CHAPTER FIFTEEN

"Control room one to control room two, come in."

Stone moved out of his chair from where he was viewing Jess' nightmare.

"What is it?" he asked.

"We have company, sir. The girl's friends have arrived."

"Excellent," Stone said.

"There is more, sir. The link has been comprised. With them are a small group of avatars."

Stone cursed.

"Do you know how many of our followers came through?"

"Over three hundred at last count, sir."

"Start attacking them."

"Yes, sir. Control room one, out."

"It would seem our other guests have arrived," Stone said out loud.

"Should we also go welcome them?" Deli asked.

Stone looked at the monitor that was showing bits and pieces of Jess' nightmare.

"I guess I can catch the show later. Trisha, would you like to join us in welcoming our new guests?"

Trisha looked at her sister, Kim.

"You'll be okay here, right?"

"I was the last time you left me, remember?"

"Fine, stay here."

Turning her attention to Stone, she said, "I'm in. Let's go."

"There they are," Bobby said, pointing in the direction of the kids.

"I see them," Liz said, "But who or what are the others?"

"They are avatars. They are here to help them."

"Avatars?" Liz asked. "What is that?"

Bobby smiled.

"An Avatar is a cartoon person for the internet. A personalized video game character."

"Oh, I see. But how are they able to help?" Liz asked, still a bit confused.

"Satan linked this world to the internet, allowing many more to join in on his evil plan. You had fainted just before that could be explained to you. That is what they were trying to show you."

Liz nodded.

"I'm in the Lord's army!"

Liz turned her head.

"Where is that coming from?" Liz asked.

"It would seem that they have announced themselves with a song," Bobby replied.

"But where is it coming from?"

Bobby pointed to the hovering speaker in the air.

"That young man, Tim, launched that speaker device into the air to praise the Lord, and have something nice to listen to in this place."

"But," Liz said, "What about the element of surprise?"

Bobby looked at her.

"Liz," he said, taking her hand. "They already knew Jessica's friends were coming."

"That doesn't make me feel any better."

"I know it doesn't."

Liz looked straight at Bobby.

"Would you pray with me?"

Bobby smiled and said, "I'd be honored too."

Liz knelt down on her knees.

Bobby joined her.

"Lord, please protect Jessica. Watch over her friends and those who are helping them as well. Give me Your strength, Lord, to get through this. I pray this in Jesus' Holy name, Amen."

"Amen," Bobby said.

Liz gave Bobby a hug.

"Thank you," she whispered in his ear.

Satan, in the form of a dragon, flew through the sky, watching as the group advanced closer toward the fortress.

"I see you have finally arrived," he said to himself.

"How would one of you like to join me up on the roof?"

He looked to see which one he wanted. After he made his decision, he dove in.

"I don't get it," Plate said. "We've announced ourselves with Tim's music player. I thought we would have had some action by now."

"Keep your guard up," Michael said. "We could be attacked any moment now."

"I still don't see- whoa!"

Before Plate could finish his sentence, a red dragon flew from behind them, just a few feet over their heads.

"Look at the wingspan on that thing!" Plate said after it flew by.

"It's coming back again!" Ashley yelled, aiming her crossbow at it.

As the dragon got closer, Ashley took the shot.

The arrow bounced off the mammoth creature.

"Uh-oh. Not good," she said as the dragon flew over their heads a second time.

"Take cover!" Michael said as he and Theron drew their swords.

As the dragon came around the third time, the angels stood ready.

"Fools!" The dragon said.

The dragon flew in, this time grabbing Tim with its claws.

But not before Michael and Theron were able to hit the beast's underbelly.

The dragon screamed and flew away.

"Tim!" Ashley yelled.

Ashley looked at Michael and Theron and said, "We have to do something! We have to go get him!"

Michael looked at Theron and said, "Go!"

Wings appeared from Theron's back, as he took flight.

"Plate?" John said, "It looks like the action you wanted just arrived."

Coming in fast were ninjas, humans, and a variety of mythological creatures.

"Let go of me!" Tim said, trying to release the grip of the dragon holding him.

The dragon growled.

Tim noticed that the dragon was taking him to the large fortress.

Oh, please let me find Jess, Tim prayed.

Without warning, the dragon dropped him on the roof.

Stunned, Tim shook his head.

The dragon shifted into human form wearing a tuxedo.

"Nice of you to drop by," the man said.

"I didn't have much of a choice, now did I?" Tim shot back.

Who is this guy?

"No, no. I guess not."

"Who are you, anyway?" Tim asked.

"You may call me Lucifer."

Satan? Oh, great.

Just as Tim was about to reply, Theron flew in and stood at the edge.

"Ah, Theron," Lucifer said. "It's been such a long time."

"Not long enough, Satan."

"Have you come to interrupt my meeting with this young man?"

Theron, wings still outstretched, crossed his arms.

"When I get word to do so, yes," came his reply.

Lucifer laughed.

"Ah, Theron. Still having to have your hand held in every situation, I see."

Theron said nothing.

What a jerk.

"Well, I have no problem with your eavesdropping. For the moment, anyway."

Lucifer walked over to a table and sat down.

"Care to join me?" Lucifer asked. "The steak is quite good."

You've got to be kidding.

Tim crossed his arms.

"Where is Jessica?"

Lucifer grabbed a fork and knife and began cutting into his steak.

"All in good time, my boy."

Not your "boy."

Lucifer put the fork to his mouth and bit into the steak.

"Hmm. This is really good. Are you sure you don't want to try a piece?"

Tim said nothing.

After Lucifer finished chewing, he said, "Now for the reason I brought you here: I want you to join me."

"No way, Satan!" Tim said.

"And why not?" Lucifer asked, taking another bite.

"Because you are an evil liar."

"Am I now? Who told you that?"

"The Bible."

Lucifer wiped his mouth with a napkin and laughed.

"The Bible? My boy, that is only one side of the story, and it's not even accurate!"

"Enough of your lies, Satan. Where is Jess?"

Lucifer stood.

"Join me and you can see her. Renounce your God, like your friend has and you can see her."

"There is no way Jess would join you!"

"No? You have no idea what she has gone through. This God of yours abandoned her. She belongs to me now! Renounce Him, and you can see her."

Oh, God, be with Jess. Watch over her and protect her.

"No, Satan. Jess is strong. The fact that I would have to renounce my faith to see her lets me believe she hasn't caved into your lies."

Lucifer laughed.

"You silly fool! Your faith in your God will be her undoing! Renounce Him and I will let her go!"

"I rebuke you, Satan! In the name of my Lord Jesus Christ! Be gone from me!"

Lucifer was thrown by an invisible force off the roof.

While in mid-air, he changed into the form of the dragon.

"Your friend will pay dearly for this!" Lucifer yelled as he flew away.

As Tim watched Lucifer fly away, Theron came to his side.

"What do I do now?" Tim asked. "Should I go find Jess myself, since I'm here, or do I go back and stand with my friends?"

"I cannot answer that for you. I am sorry."

Tim walked to the edge and looked.

He saw his friends in battle.

"I have to help them," he said, pressing a button on his suit.

A small jet pack emerged from his back.

"Let's get going," Tim said as he jumped off the roof and flew in the air.

Plate looked around and said, "This looks like every season of 'Power Rangers' combined!"

"I don't think they will be as easy to fight as the Putty's were in the first few seasons, Plate," John replied.

"Who knows? They might be," Plate said with a grin.

The advancing mob of evil stopped twenty feet away, surrounding the group in a semi-circle.

Everything was quiet for a half minute.

Finally, a man clothed like a samurai stepped forward and spoke.

"For what reason do you come here?"

Not knowing who should address the Samurai, John looked at Michael. Michael looked at John and nodded. He stepped forward and said, "We have come to free our imprisoned friend."

"So," the Samurai said, "you are the warriors sent by the Shining King?"

"'The Shining King?'" John asked.

"That's what God's name is in here," J9M said. "God is the Shining King, and Satan is the Dark Master. The girl, Jessica, is the Shining King's Daughter."

John shook his head and addressed the Samurai.

"Yes. We are the warriors of the Shining King! We are here to bring His Daughter back home."

"That will not be so easy," the Samurai said. "For you will have to face me, Ling Yang, and my associates here," he said spreading his arms wide.

John looked at his group and then turned his attention back to the samurai, Ling Yang. John lifted his sword and said, "Bring it."

Ling looked offended and pulled his sword.

"Attack!" He yelled.

"Here we go!" Plate said, activating his laser whip.

"Spread out!" John yelled, just as Ling's sword connected with his shield.

John stepped back, swinging his sword in the direction of the samurai, connecting with his sword.

"Do you really think you and your friends can make your way past us to rescue your friend? You are outnumbered!"

"'For we walk by faith, not by sight!'" John said, sweep kicking Ling's legs out from under him.

Ling fell, but quickly recovered, making a rolling stand.

"It won't be that easy, I can assure you," Ling said.

"Nothing in life comes easy," John shot back.

"True, very true," Ling said, bringing his sword down.

John brought his shield up and swung his sword at Ling's leg.

Thunk!

"Ah!" Ling said, stepping back.

John looked at Ling's leg and saw sparks flying from the wound.

"You- you're a robot!" John said.

Ling laughed.

"Expect the unexpected, kid!" Ling said as he swung his sword at him.

John dodged the attack with his shield, spun around, and caught Ling's back with his sword.

Thunk!

"Ah!" Ling said again.

Sparks flew from his back.

"Are you really programmed for pain, or are you just playing me?" John asked.

"Wouldn't you like to know?" Ling said with a grin.

"John! Behind you!" he heard Sarah scream.

John spun around to see an ape running at him.

The beast jumped on John, causing both of them to fall to the ground.

John used the momentum to launch the ape over and off him.

He heard the ape connect with something.

As he got up, he saw that it had landed on Ling.

The Ape rolled off Ling, sparks flying from its chest, Ling's sword imbedded.

"Bravo," Ling said getting up, his right arm dangling, sparks flying.

"I'd give you applause, but sadly, I have no use of one of my arms."

John looked at Ling.

"Are all of you robots?" He asked.

Ling gave a shrug.

"There is really only one way to find out, now isn't there?" He said, as he ripped off his dangling arm and swung it at John.

John dodged the robotic arm and swung his sword just under his shield.

Thunk!

"Ah!" Ling said.

"Now I know you're playing me," John said as he watched sparks fly from the robot's mid-section.

"You didn't scream when your arm was dangling or when you ripped it off."

Ling laughed.

"Quite right," he said, attacking with his arm yet again.

John circled and the handle of his sword struck Ling's head.

"Ah- ah- ah!" The robot yelled out.

"Is-s-s th-that th-the b-b-best y-y-you c-c-can do?" Ling said, falling to the ground.

"Th-this is n-n-not ov-over..."

"Shut up," John said walking over and removing the robot's head from its body with his sword.

"W-we w-will w-win," the head continued talking.

"Figures," John said to himself as he picked up the head.

John tossed the head up and swung his sword like a baseball bat connecting on the first try.

The head flew and hit the head of a ninja fighting with Sarah, knocking the ninja out.

The head gave a tiny explosion.

Sarah looked in the direction of where the head came from.

"Payback for the ape!" John shouted.

Sarah smiled and went off to help Ashley fight a strange creature.

John ran over and started fighting alongside Plate.

"Did I miss anything?" John asked as he dodged a blow to his ribs.

"Not much," Plate said, swinging his whip "I feel like Indiana Jones, though. Where have you been?"

"I just got done fighting that samurai. He was a robot, by the way."

"Figures," Plate said, swinging his whip out from under the ninja's feet.

"So far, everything here, except the ninjas, are robots. The ninjas disappear after about a half minute of being down."

"Avatars?" John asked.

"Looks like it," Plate said.

Something in the air caught John's attention.

"Hey! Look, it's Tim! He's coming back!"

Plate finished whipping another assailant and looked up.

"Hey, you're right! I wonder what happened?"

"We can find out later, but right now, we have more important things to deal with," John said.

At that moment, a barbarian swung his sword at John's head.

John caught the sword with his own.

"Great," Plate said, swinging his whip around the barbarian's legs.

"Now we have to fight Conan!"

As the barbarian fell, John swung his sword, separating the barbarian's head from his body.

Sparks flew as the head rolled away.

CHAPTER SIXTEEN

When Ashley heard John yell, "Spread out!" she didn't know which way to go.

She backed up a little when she saw an ape running toward her.

She aimed her crossbows at its feet and fired.

The arrows lodged into the ape's feet and the ground.

Sparks came flying from its imprisoned feet.

"Robots!" Ashley exclaimed, relieved they weren't real.

Ashley added two more arrows to the mechanical ape, one to the chest, and the other to the head.

The ape dropped to the ground and exploded.

"Thank You, Lord!" Ashley said out loud.

Ashley started firing on every ape she saw, cutting them down, two by two.

Suddenly, a strange creature appeared in front of her.

The creature stood 8 feet tall, with four arms, three legs, and five eyes, two on either side of its head and one in the middle. Its mouth had razor-sharp teeth.

"Oh, boy," Ashley said, looking up at it.

Not knowing what else to do, Ashley fired her arrows at it.

One arrow hit the creature's neck and stayed there. It didn't appear to be fazed by it at all.

"Uh-oh," Ashley said as the creature's mammoth-sized arms came falling down toward her.

Ashley rolled out of the way just in time. When she regained her footing, she saw a crater-sized hole where she had once stood.

The monster looked at her and snarled.

"You wouldn't be a misunderstood creature, would you?"

The monster opened its mouth and hissed.

"I guess not," she said, aiming her crossbow at it again and firing.

One of the arrows caught one of its eyes on the right side.

The monster screamed a horrible scream and Ashley fell to the ground in terror.

With its four remaining good eyes, the monster lifted its arms once again.

Ashley, frozen in fear, cowered, wishing she was invisible.

"God, help me!" she cried out loud.

Suddenly, the monster looked confused.

"Hey! Pick on someone your own size!" Sarah yelled, a sword extending out of her suit.

Sarah swung her sword, hitting one of the monster's arms.

The monster gave an almost ear-splitting scream.

The arm disappeared as it left the monster's body.

"Next!" Sarah yelled as she hit its leg with her sword.

The monster screamed again, weaker than before, falling to the ground.

Ashley, recovering slightly, drew her crossbows and fired off four more shots at the remaining eyes.

The monster's scream was muffled, almost like it had gone hoarse.

Sarah finished the creature off, placing her sword in its skull.

Within seconds, the monster disappeared.

Sarah turned to Ashley and said, "How'd you do that?"

"Do what?"

"Turn completely invisible! I thought the suit only changed colors!"

"Wait a minute," Ashley said, raising her crossbows and dropping two more apes behind Sarah.

Sarah turned around to see the apes fall.

"Okay..." she said, turning back to Ashley.

"I what?" Ashley asked.

"You turned invisible. Just after you fell."

"I did? I didn't notice," she said, shooting another ape.

"Listen, I don't know how I did it. It was either the suit, or it was God, probably both. Right now, we haven't got time to figure it out. Let's go help the others."

"Okay, let's go," Sarah said.

"Hang on," Ashley said.

"What?" Sarah asked, facing Ashley.

"Am I invisible again?" she asked.

Sarah smiled. "Yep, you sure are. Although, I can make you out, you know, like how they do it on TV."

"Perfect! Let's go."

"Hey!" Sarah said, looking up. "Tim's back!"

Ashley looked up, too.

"Good. We could use his help," she said, firing an arrow at a charging barbarian.

As Tim flew to where his friends were, he saw Michael helping out the E.C.H. avatars.

The military were holding their own.

As he was flying in, he was firing off the laser that was attached to both his arms.

As Tim landed, there were only a few remaining moving targets left.

A few of the last remaining bad guys were in white armor, carrying swords.

Great, Tim thought. *Generic Storm Troopers with swords.*

Tim put away his lasers and drew out his claws from the back of his hands. He drew them out a foot and charged the white armored attackers. Sparks flew everywhere as Tim hit everything in his path. The "Storm Troopers" never had a chance to use their weapons.

Every last one of them fell to the ground as Tim retracted his claws.

"Tim!" Ashley yelled running up to him. "Are you okay? What happened?"

The rest of the group gathered around him.

Michael and Theron stood side by side a few feet away.

"Hey," Tim said to J9M's group, "Are you guys okay? I see that your energy bars are a little low."

"We're fine," J9M said "If we get blasted out, we'll come back in."

"If you can," Tim said.

"Yeah," J9M agreed. "If we can."

"Tim," John said, "what happened? Where'd you go?"

"That dragon that took me was Satan. He wanted a meeting with me. He took me to the roof of the building and said if I renounced God, I could see Jess.

"I refused."

"Good," John said.

"Wait a minute," Ashley said, "You were on the roof, and you came back?"

"I felt I had to," Tim said.

Ashley gave him a hug.

"Thanks, we needed you here, anyway. I'm sure that was still a tough decision for you to make."

"Yes, it was," Tim replied.

"I think we should get going before we run into any more trouble out here," John said.

"I at least want to make it a few yards closer before anything else happens"

"You and me both," Plate said.

Growing weary of looking at the screen, Pastor Stevens got up and let Maggie take over the computer.

"In just a few seconds, we will be able to view what's going on in there," Maggie said.

"Good," Jack said, "this waiting is making me nervous."

Jeff came over with a couple of chairs for Jack and Pastor Stevens.

"Here, take a seat. I'm sure we'll all want to sit down once we see what's going on."

Both Jack and Pastor Stevens grabbed the chairs from Jeff.

"Yeah, thanks. You might be right," Pastor Stevens said.

"Alright," Maggie said. "I'm in. I picked the appearance of that of a small bug. We should be able to see what's going on, and they shouldn't see us."

"Then I suggest that you stay as far away as the little camera will let you," Jack said.

"We want to see what's going on in there without our little gizmo getting broke, don't we?"

"Yep. Exactly," Maggie said. "I'll keep my distance if I can."

"So," Jeff said. "What do you think is in there?"

"We're about to find out," Maggie replied. "And we are in!"

"Good grief!" Jeff said. "Are those...apes?"

"And ninjas," Maggie said. "Along with a few other things."

"You have got to be kidding me," Jack said.

"I don't see Tim or Theron anywhere," Pastor Stevens said. "Do any of you?"

"Nope," Maggie said. "But I do see other people helping the kids fight."

"Must be from the open link," Jack said.

"Yeah," Jeff said. "Some of them look like they are military. Friends of yours, Jack?"

Jack took a better look at the screen.

"They could be. I don't recognize anyone there."

"Check out that monster Ashley's fighting with!" Maggie said.

"It's huge!"

"My goodness," Pastor Stevens said. "How tall is that thing?"

"Given Ashley's size, I'd say between seven and ten feet."

Jack let out a whistle.

"I'd hate to come across that thing in a dark alley," Jeff commented.

"You and me both, brother," Jack said. "You and me both."

"Maggie, can you enlarge or get us closer?" Pastor Stevens asked.

"Yeah, I think so," Maggie said, typing on the keyboard.

A few seconds later Ashley and the monster filled the screen.

"Amazing," Jack said.

They watched as Ashley got out of the way as the monster's arms came down, hitting nothing but the ground.

They all sat stunned.

The screen showed a huge hole where the monster's arms had just been.

"Incredible!" Jeff said as he watched the screen.

They watched as Ashley fired her crossbow at the monster and then fell to the ground.

"Oh, no!" Maggie said.

They watched the monster raise its arms once more.

"Oh, God, be with her!" Pastor Stevens prayed out loud.

Suddenly, without warning, Ashley disappeared, and the monster stood, confused.

"What...what just happened?" Jeff asked. "Where's Ashley?"

"Right there!" Maggie said, pointing at the screen. "She's invisible, but I can make out her outline!"

"The monster doesn't see her!" Pastor Stevens said.

"Praise God!"

They watched as Sarah came to the aid of Ashley and watched as they both put the monster down.

"Thank You, Jesus," Pastor Stevens prayed.

"Amen," Jack said.

"How long do we wait?" Trisha asked, standing outside the fortress.

Stone stood, watching. "We wait until they come within a few yards of us, then we strike."

"That's a long way off," Trisha replied.

Stone stared at her.

"Then might I suggest you go take a ride?"

Trisha looked at him, confused.

"What do you mean?" she asked.

Stone pointed to the crystal around her neck.

"Remember what I told you about that crystal? I told you that you have control over all the creatures here. Take a ride. I don't care if it's on a land creature or one from the air. Ride around the building, I'm sure you'll enjoy it."

Trisha looked doubtfully at the crystal around her neck and touched it with her figures.

"How?" Trisha asked.

"Just call upon them. Land or air, it doesn't matter."

"Alright," Trisha said, closing her eyes. "I call upon the riding creatures of this world, both land and air."

Trisha opened her eyes and gasped.

There in front and surrounding her were a huge gathering of both land and air creatures, waiting.

"Wow," Trisha said, taking the scene in. "Amazing."

"Which will it be? Land or air?"

"I-I've never flown before," Trisha said. "The closest thing, I guess would have been when I went on a roller coaster a couple of years back."

"So, what do you choose?" Stone asked.

"I guess... I'll take to the air."

"Splendid," Stone said, raising his arm and dropping it.

Instantly, the land creatures scattered.

Amazed, Trisha looked at Stone and asked, "How'd you do that?"

Stone gave a slight smile and said, "My secret. Now, which one of these magnificent beasts do you want to ride?"

"May I suggest," Deli said, stepping forward, "you ride the unicorn? I know you humans are fascinated with these creatures."

Trisha looked at the many creatures. Many seemed way too big to ride and others looked too mean.

"Yes, Deli, thank you," Trisha said. "The unicorn sounds great."

"Perfect," Stone said. "Just call it."

"Okay," Trisha said to herself as she put her hand around the crystal once more.

"Unicorn, come to me. You others may go."

Trisha opened her eyes and saw a single row of unicorns and laughed.

"I guessed I should have realized there would have been more than one unicorn."

Trisha looked at the unicorns.

The color of the unicorn's horns differed. Some were red, others white, grey, brown, blue, and purple. One was even a rainbow color. The unicorn's colors were different, also. Some were golden with red hair; others were black and white with blue hair. Some were just plain black with white hair, and vice versa.

"They're beautiful!" Trisha said, walking by and examining them.

"Ever ride a horse?" Deli asked.

"Yeah, when I was at my aunt's ranch, I was ten." Trisha told her.

"This will be kind of like that," Deli replied.

Trisha smiled. "I kinda knew that. Thanks."

Trisha stopped when she came to the unicorn with the rainbow horn.

She touched the horn and said, "You're beautiful. I love the color of your horn. May I ride you?"

Yes, you may.

Trisha jumped back. "Did you...just talk?"

The crystal around your neck allows us to communicate with each other. Didn't Mr. Stone tell you that?

Trisha looked at Stone and touched her crystal.

"I-I don't know. I may have forgotten," Trisha said.

Looking at Stone, she said, "I can't believe I'm communicating with a unicorn!"

"Why should any of this surprise you anymore, Miss Conner?" Stone asked.

"I...I'm not sure. I'm just not used to this, I guess."

"Give it time," Stone said.

Touching the crystal once more, Trisha said, "I have found the one I want to ride. The rest of your unicorns may go. Thanks."

Without hesitation, the unicorns flew away.

"Beautiful," Trisha said, looking in the air.

I'm glad you approve, the unicorn said.

Trisha looked back at the unicorn.

"What is your name?" She asked.

You may call me Airborne.

"Airborne?" Trisha said. "That's a nice name. I like it. My name is Trisha."

Pleased to meet you, my dear, Airborne said, giving a little bow.

Trisha giggled.

"Are you ready to take flight?" Stone asked, walking over.

"Yes, I believe I am. What about you, Airborne?"

Whenever you are ready, my dear.

Trisha smiled. "Yeah, we're ready."

"Good, hop on and enjoy the ride," Stone replied.

After Trisha got on, she said, "Okay, boy. I'm ready when you are."

Without saying a word, Airborne flapped his mighty wings and flew off.

"Whoa!" Trisha yelled.

Is everything alright, mi' lady?

"Uh, yeah," Trisha said, regaining her composure.

"It's just that I've never really flown before. I'm not used to it."

Do not worry. You will be fine. So, where do you want me to take you?

"Um, just around this building, thanks. Just circle it for a while."

As you wish.

As the unicorn flew, Trisha let the wind blow through her hair.

"This is amazing! I just feel so free!" she said.

I'm glad you are enjoying yourself.

"You are so lucky you can fly; this is great!"

Thank you, I guess because I can do it, I take it for granted.

"The view up here is spectacular!"

Yes, it is. I may take flying for granted, but the view never gets old.

Trisha closed her eyes and felt the wind blow on her face.

After a few more minutes of flying, Trisha said, "Okay, Airborne, I'm ready to land."

As you wish.

The unicorn slowly descended.

When they were on the ground, Trisha whispered in Airborne's ear, "Thank you for a magnificent flight."

Anytime, my dear.

"So," Stone asked, "how was it?"

"Oh, it was unbelievably amazing! It was absolutely incredible!"

"I think she may have enjoyed it," Deli said to Stone.

"Oh, without a doubt!" Trisha said.

If you enjoyed that, would you like to see how I ride on land?

"Absolutely!" Trisha said.

The unicorn took off in a gallop, with Trisha holding on, laughing.

CHAPTER SEVENTEEN

Kim remembered waking up in blackness, alone.

"Hello?" Kim had called out. "Is anyone there?"

"Well, look who finally awoke," a voice had said.

"Hello? Who are you? Where am I?"

The voice laughed a harsh laugh.

"We are in your subconscious. Usually, I would keep my hosts unconscious, completely unaware, but I thought I'd like to have some fun with you."

"What...what do you mean?" Kim asked. "Who are you?"

A dim light had appeared out of nowhere and Kim saw a figure step out in front of her.

Kim gasped. She was looking at herself!

"What is this? Who are you?" she had asked.

"Why, I'm you, at least for now," the other Kim laughed.

"I don't get it. This must be a nightmare. That's what it is. Just a nightmare, I'm just dreaming."

"You are half right. This is a nightmare, but you are not dreaming."

Kim looked shocked and confused.

The other Kim laughed.

"Don't you get it, yet, human? You've just been possessed! I have taken over your body!"

"What?" Kim had yelled. "But how?"

"With that chant Stone had you repeat. I'd love to stay and chat, but I've got business to take care of. Don't go anywhere," she had said with a laugh.

"What? Wait!" Kim cried.

The light had vanished, and Kim had been alone in the dark again.

All she could do was listen as the demon started and continued to torment the girl, Jessica.

She had cried out repeatedly, trying to get the demon to stop harassing Jessica, but it was like the demon didn't hear.

She had even tried to call out when her sister and the demon were talking.

"Trisha! That's not me talking with you! Trisha, help me!"

But it was to no avail.

She had just about given up when she heard Jessica yelling at what was called The Shadows.

"In the Name of Jesus, get away from me!" she had heard her say.

Suddenly, she felt a veil lift and she could see. It happened in a blink of an eye, then she was back in darkness. She had seen the girl Jessica and what she assumed were The Shadows.

"Wh-what just happened?" she had asked.

"Shut up!" The demon had said, directing her attention back to Kim.

"Oh, God, help me!" Kim cried.

"God?" the demon had yelled. "It's too late for God to help you now! You're mine!"

Before Kim could say anything else, she lost consciousness.

When she awoke, the demon said, "Time for some more fun. I want to enjoy this, and I want you to suffer."

"Please! Please let go of me! Let me have my body back! I didn't ask for this!"

"No? You called me in. You asked me to come."

"I didn't know what I was saying. I didn't mean it! Let me go!"

"Tsk, tsk, tsk. You ought to know better than to repeat words you don't understand."

Kim cried, "Just let me go! I don't want any part in this!"

"Oh, my dear," the demon said, "You are a part of this. There is no changing that."

"Why are you doing this to me? Why are you doing this to Jessica?"

"Simple: It's fun. Right now, I'm watching Jessica have a horrible nightmare. Ah, it's wonderful, really."

"Oh, God," Kim tried to pray.

Kim felt a slap to the head.

"What did I tell you about that? God isn't going to help you!"

Kim started to cry.

The demon laughed.

"Face it, you're stuck with me!"

"Won't you tell me your name then?"

The demon laughed again.

"Oh, I guess I could do that. My name is Bal'ack."

"Please, Bal'ack, won't you let me go?"

"Yes, I will."

"You will?" Kim asked, surprised.

"Sure," Bal'ack said. "When I'm done here, I'll let you go... jump in the river, off a building, onto train tracks, the possibilities are endless!"

Bal'ack laughed.

"You're not going to let me live without you, are you?" Kim asked, near panic.

"As it stands right now, no," Bal'ack said, laughing again.

Kim started crying again.

"Oh, but look on the bright side," Bal'ack said, "Your strength has increased considerably, and you can now understand different languages."

"That doesn't help me if I don't have any control over my own body!" Kim yelled.

"Ha! You're right! Too bad, so sad!" The demon laughed again.

"Please," Kim pleaded, "If you won't let me go, let Jessica go. What has she done to you?"

"I do not need a reason to do what I am called to do. I just do it, and I enjoy every minute of it!"

For the first time, Kim noticed it was quiet.

"Where is everyone?"

"Like I said, Miss Jessica is asleep having a nightmare. Your sister, Mr. Stone, and Deli went outside to welcome our visitors. Jessica's friends have arrived to rescue her as part of my master's game."

"Good, so there is a chance of Jessica getting out of here," Kim replied.

Bal'ack laughed. "Not much of one, I can assure you. We will crush her friends!"

"God, be with her friends," Kim said.

"What did I say about that!" Bal'ack shouted.

Kim felt a slap to the face, harder than the one before.

"God can't hear you! How many times do I have to tell you that, you stupid child?"

Kim started crying again.

"Leave me alone! Please! Let me go!"

Bal'ack laughed.

"Look out!" John said as four rhino-looking creatures came stampeding out of nowhere.

The creatures looked like rhinos, except the creature's skin was green, and had a three-foot-long spiked tail.

Riding upon these creatures were humanoid lizards dressed as warriors.

"You have got to be kidding me," Plate said in disbelief.

"Could this get any weirder?"

"Yes," Ashley said, looking up.

Plate looked up to see what Ashley saw.

In the sky, on four unicorns, sat humanoid turtles, also dressed like warriors.

"What is this," Plate asked, "the reptile brigade?"

"Must be," J9M said. "Nothing should be surprising anymore."

"You got that right!" John said.

"All we need now is Master Splinter," Plate said.

"Plate...," John said

"I'm just saying," Plate said.

The unicorns landed by the rhinos, and one of the lizards spoke.

"You there! What business do you have here?"

"We are here to rescue the Shining King's daughter," John said.

"Step aside, and we will do you no harm."

The lizard laughed.

"Do us no harm? Ha! You are trespassing! Turn back now and we will let you live."

"I'm afraid I can't do that, sir. We have come this far, and you will not stop us."

"Really?" The lizard said as the turtles dismounted their unicorns.

"Do you really think you can defeat us?" he asked with a laugh.

"With God, all things are possible," John said.

The lizard stopped laughing.

"God? How dare you defile my land with that name!"

The lizard drew his sword.

"Attack!" The lizard yelled.

The unicorns flew in the air while, with weapons drawn, the turtles attacked.

As a sword came down on John's shield, he kicked one of the turtle's legs out from under him.

The turtle fell and used its shell to spin, knocking John down, as well.

The turtle stood and brought his sword down.

John raised his shield for protection.

Because he was on the ground, the force of the impact knocked the wind out of him.

The turtle raised his arms again, ready to strike another blow.

John braced himself.

As the sword came down, it was pulled out of the attacker's hands by Plate's whip.

The turtle looked at Plate.

Seeing that his attacker was distracted, John kicked him between the legs.

The turtle let out a groan and backed away and went to his knees.

John got to his feet and looked from Plate, to the turtle and back to Plate.

"I didn't know if it would work. Looks like all males are the same. Thanks."

"No problem," Plate said as he used his whip to launch another turtle into the air.

"But it looks like they aren't as easily defeated as the last things we fought."

John nodded and turned his attention back to the turtle.

"Get up and fight," John said.

The turtle looked up and said, "As you wish," pulling out a small sword and attacking.

John dodged the sword and swung his sword on the turtle's arm.

The turtle screamed and cursed.

"You broke my arm!" he cried.

"I guess you're lucky you had some armor on, huh?"

Unarmed and wounded, the turtle jumped at John.

John turned and used the handle of his sword to hit the back of the turtle's head.

The turtle fell to the ground, unconscious.

John left the turtle and went to help Plate, who was now using his whip in sword mode on a turtle with a mace and shield.

"Mind if I join you?" John asked.

"Be my guest," Plate said, ducking the swing of the turtle's mace.

As the mace came down, John swung his sword, separating the turtle's hand from his wrist.

The turtle screamed in agony and spewed venomous words at the two humans.

"Be quiet!" John said, taking the turtle's head off.

The turtle's head landed with a sickening thud.

"Uhhh...." was the final sound to come from the turtle's lips.

John shuttered.

"I hope these aren't real-life forms."

"They don't bleed," Plate offered.

"Thank God for that," John said.

John turned around in time to see the other two turtles fall, then turned his attention to the leader lizard.

"May we pass through? Or do we have to face you also?"

The lizards dismounted and the leader said, "You fought well against my comrades, young man. Now you must face us!"

The lizard raised his sword in the air and brought it down.

"Now!" The lizard leader yelled.

The rhinos were the first to attack. They charged and everyone had to dodge out of the way.

When John stood, the Lizard leader attacked his sword, connecting with John's sword.

"You could have made this easy on yourself, boy," the lizard said.

"All you had to do was go back the way you came. Of course, I do love a good fight every now and then."

"I'm here for a friend and you are not going to stop me!" John said.

"You petty humans and your friendships!" the lizard spat.

"You and your friends will fall!"

"Only if it's God's will, and I don't believe it is," John shot back.

The lizard snarled and knocked John's legs out from under him with his tail.

John groaned.

"Your God is not as powerful as you think!" The lizard said, bringing his sword down.

John rolled and stood.

"Now if that were true," he said, "why would His name upset you so much?"

"Shut up!" The lizard said.

"I think you know how real He is, and you don't want to face it. Am I close?"

"Shut up, shut up, you stupid human!"

"He is more powerful than I could ever dream of," John said.

"Shut up!" the lizard said, swinging his tail in the direction of John's head.

John moved and cut the lizard's tail.

"Ah!" The lizard turned, rage in his eyes. "You will pay for that!"

"Sorry, I left my wallet at my church, do you take IOUs?"

In a blind rage, the lizard ran at John. John stuck his sword out, ramming it into his chest.

The lizard fell limp as John pulled his sword out of the creature's chest.

"John! Duck!"

Without hesitation, John ducked and covered his head with his shield.

The body of another lizard fell right by him.

John looked up and saw Tim, his arm still outstretched with his laser gun.

"Thanks," John said.

"No problem," Tim said, putting his arm down.

John looked around.

All the lizards and turtles were on the ground, unmoving.

"Where are the rhinos?" John asked.

"They disappeared after they were hit three or four times with a laser," Time replied.

"Oh, okay. I think I like it better when they do that, or sparks fly from 'em."

"Yeah, me too," Plate said, coming over.

"Is everyone alright?" John asked.

"I think we lost a few of the E.C.H's. The rhinos really tossed some of them for a loop."

"Oh, man," John said. "How many are there?"

"Three, but don't worry," J9M said, walking over. "The system just locked them out, they're fine in the real world."

"Well, that's good to know, I guess," John said.

"Oh, and half of Tank's team got sent back to the real world as well," J9M offered.

"Let me guess, the rhinos took them out, too?" Tim asked.

"You got it."

"Hey, Tank!" John called. "Do you know how your guys are? The ones that were hit by the rhinos?"

"I don't know," Tank said, "they should be fine, but the way our systems are made, they may have a pretty good headache."

"I hope that's all they have," John said, "and I hope it goes away fast for them."

"Thanks," Tank replied.

Theron walked over and said, "Tank, your friends are fine. They are fatigued, but they are fine."

"Thanks, that's good to know."

"Hey, we're almost there," Plate said. "I hope we can get there without any more interruptions."

"Don't count on it," Michael replied.

"Hey, I can dream, can't I?"

"Hey, look at this!" Sarah yelled.

The group turned and saw Sarah and Ashley on two of the four unicorns.

"Sarah! Ashley! Get off those things!" John yelled, running over to them.

"Relax, John," Sarah said, petting the mythical horse.

"They are very friendly."

"But those turtles were riding these things!" John said.

"That doesn't mean they are evil," Sarah countered. "They didn't attack us like the rhinos did. They stayed in the air. Besides, in those Western movies, just because the bad guy is riding a horse, that doesn't make the horse bad, does it? Aren't unicorns good in mythology?"

"Right now," John said, "I can't even remember."

John looked at the unicorn; the unicorn looked back.

Do not judge us for what others do.

John blinked. "What?"

"What?" Sarah asked.

"I think this unicorn just spoke to me!"

"Really?" Ashley said. "What did it say?"

"'Do not judge us for what others do,'" John replied

"That's amazing, John," Sarah said with a smile. "I think he likes you."

Let us carry you as far as you need to go.

"Michael, Theron," John asked, "Are you hearing this one talk?"

"Yes, John," Michael said. "I can hear what this one is saying."

"Is this a trick?" he asked the archangel.

"It is not," Michael assured him. "The Almighty has seen fit to turn the tables on Satan, using these creatures to benefit you and your friends."

"Okay," John said. "Sarah, can I ride this one?"

"Sure," she said, dismounting the unicorn.

As John got on the back of the mythical horse, he asked the avatars, "Are you guys okay, walking I mean?"

"We're not really here, man," J9M said. "We're fine."

"The same goes for us," Tank said. "Enjoy the ride."

As Plate hopped on the other unicorn, John looked at Tim.

"Are you okay, Tim?" John asked.

"Yeah, Tim," Ashley asked. "Do you want to ride with me?"

"Actually, guys, I'm fine. This suit doesn't even make me feel like I'm walking, and yet I walk just fine."

"Okay, then," John said.

Turning his attention to the unicorn, he asked, "What do I call you?"

You may call me Gemstone.

"Well, Gemstone, are we walking, or are we flying?"

Let us walk so the others can keep up.

"Good idea," John said. "Let's ride!"

Jack stood up. "I'm gonna go see if I can get through and find out how those military boys are after being knocked out of there."

"Good idea, Jack," Maggie said. "Those rhino...things really hit them hard."

"They weren't really there," Jeff said, "but who knows how that affected them."

"Exactly," Jack said, punching a few buttons on his phone. "Excuse me."

The phone rang once.

"Password, please," the voice on the other end said.

Jack sighed.

"Screwtape."

"Hello, Jack. Enjoying the show? Your friends are doing rather well, aren't they?"

Jack ignored the comment and said, "I'm calling to find out how your boys are doing after tangling with a bunch of green rhinos."

"They are fine. No physical damage if that is what you're asking?"

"What about mentally?" Jack asked.

"They are mentally and physically fatigued. Nothing permanent, I can assure you."

"Did the medics tell you that or is that just your opinion?"

"A quick overview was done as soon as they came out," the voice assured him.

"They are now in the infirmary getting a total workup done. Satisfied?"

"For now. Keep me posted if anything changes."

"You got it, Jack. It's been a heck of a day."

"Thanks, it sure has," Jack said just before the line went dead.

"Everything alright?" Jeff asked as Jack came walking back.

"They are being checked out now as we speak,"

Jack replied. "So far, everything seems to be fine."

"Thank God," Pastor Stevens said.

"What did I miss?" Jack asked.

"You remember the unicorns those turtles were riding?" Maggie asked.

"Yeah?" Jack said.

"Well, four of the kids are riding them now. Plate, John, Sarah, and Ashley."

"Really?"

"See for yourself," Maggie said pointing at the screen.

Jack took a breath. "Why should I be surprised?"

"Beautiful," Ashley said.

"What is?" Tim said, walking a step behind her.

"The water," Ashley said pointing.

"Over there by the outcropping of rock."

Tim looked for a second.

"Yeah, I guess. If it wasn't swimming with who knows what and it being red."

"I don't see anything in the water, but you're right. Just pretend it's a sunset on the water."

"Okay, then," Tim said. "I see your point."

Ashley smiled. "Of course you do."

Tim laughed.

After riding in silence for a while, Ashley said, "Tim?"

"Yeah?" he asked.

"What happened to the speaker you had shot up in the air?"

"Huh," Tim said. "I completely forgot about it. I didn't realize it was gone. I still have music playing in my helmet. It must have stayed put when I was grabbed by Satan."

"Do you have another one, or could you transmit a signal to bring it back to you? I'm desperate for some Praise & Worship."

"I'll see what I can do," Tim said.

"Thanks."

"No prob."

While she was waiting for Tim's speaker, Ashley started singing "How Great Thou Art."

The others joined in as well.

"Here it comes," Tim said.

The speaker came into view and was just starting to play "I can only imagine" when it arrived.

Slowly, they approached the outcropping of rock.

"Step no further," a female voice said.

"Hello?" John called out.

A female dressed in a bronze bikini stepped out from behind the rocks. Nine similarly dressed women stepped out behind her.

Tim took in a breath.

They were all strikingly beautiful with shoulder-length blond and brown hair.

Wow! Tim thought

"Great," Ashley said. "We have Xena and Amazon Barbies to deal with now."

"I am Jolla," the leader said, "and we want your men."

Tim heard Ashley laugh.

Guess it's time for the temptation of the guys.

"Oh, let me guess. It is time for you to bear children and you want them to be the fathers?"

"Yes," Jolla said. "Stand aside, females, so we may take your men and do that which our customs allow, or we will have to kill you."

"What your customs allow?" Ashley asked, astonished.

This would be funny, Tim thought. *If it wasn't so serious.*

"I think I saw this episode on Hercules once," Plate said. "You know, the one starring Kevin Sorbo."

"Men," Jolla spoke again. "Come. We can and will fulfill your desires far better than these mere girls could ever dream of doing."

"Did she just say what I think she said?" Sarah asked.

"Yes," Ashley said, "she did."

"Sorry, girls," John spoke to Jolla and her friends.

"We have more important things to do right now than to let you have your way with us."

"But you have the most amazing eyes," Tim heard himself say.

"Tim!" Ashley said.

"What? Oh, sorry. Did I say that out loud?" Tim asked.

Stupid! Just shut up and pray!

"You there, in the strange metal armor," Jolla said referring to Tim.

Uh-oh.

"Will you come to us? All we need is one man. We will do what you desire of us."

You've got to be kidding.

Finally, Tim paid attention to his scans.

The readout said they were robots.

"No, thanks," Tim said. "I'm not into the whole robot fantasy thing."

He then added, "But whoever did your eyes did an amazing job."

What is going on? Lord, protect me!

"Tim!" Ashley said once again. "Stop it!"

Jolla looked around.

Looking at Michael and Theron, she said, "What about you two? It'll be worth your while."

The two angels declined.

"So," she said. "There is no one in your party man enough for us? Fine. You will all die!"

Without saying anything more, Jolla and the rest of the Amazonian women attacked them.

Tim raised both arms and started firing as Ashley fired off her arrows at the coming female warriors.

Yeah, less attractive when they're falling apart.

John, Plate, and Sarah were all off their unicorns, fighting with their swords and shields. What should have been a battle turned into a victory as the Amazonian women were easily defeated.

"That," John said, looking around at the fallen warriors with sparks flying everywhere, "was too easy."

"It wasn't about fighting them," Michael said, "It was about rejecting their advances toward you. Remember, I told you Satan would use anything to hinder you. That even meant the lust of the flesh."

"But they weren't even real," Plate said.

"That didn't matter," Tim said.

"Did you see their eyes?"

Plate nodded.

"It didn't matter if they were real or not. They were made to entice us off our path. Their eyes, their hair, even their bodies, man. And forgive me, but you could get lost in their eyes. I almost did!"

"Almost?" Ashley said.

"Fine, I did. I'm sorry, but I did, I couldn't even keep my mouth shut," Tim said.

"Well, it's better than looking into the eyes of Medusa or the Basilisk," Ashley said.

"What?" Tim asked. "Medusa I know, but the Basilisk?"

"It's a lizard with deadly venom and if it stares at you, it kills you."

"Have you been reading up on mythology lately?" Tim asked.

"No," Ashley said.

"Then how did you know that?" Tim said.

"I-I don't know," Ashley said.

Tim gave a light laugh. "Can't remember where you learned something. It happens."

"Are we ready to go?" John asked.

"Yeah," Tim said. "Let's go."

As they passed the rocks, a contemporary worship song played in the sky.

"What's that?" Trisha asked as she dismounted Airborne.

Sounds like singing, Airborne replied.

"But where's it coming from?"

"There," Stone said, pointing. "Our visitors have arrived."

Trisha looked to where Stone was pointing. About fifty yards away, she saw them. A total of fifteen, four of them riding unicorns and eleven walking. Two of the eleven walking looked a bit taller than the rest.

"I think it's time we welcomed them, wouldn't you say so, my dear?" Stone said, still looking in the distance.

"Uh, yeah," Trisha said, mounting her unicorn once more.

"This is gonna be fun," Deli said.

"I hope so," Stone replied, walking a few feet ahead.

When the group was within a few yards of him, Stone called out, "Hello!"

The group stopped.

"Stone," Tim said flatly

"So nice to see you again!" Stone said. "Welcome, welcome!"

"Where's Jessica?" Tim yelled.

Stone laughed.

"Ah," Stone said. "That's for us to know and you to find out."

Stone laughed again.

"Come and see if you can find her. You will have to get through us all."

Stone clapped his hands, and the sky became clouded with all sorts of flying creatures.

Out of the fortress and out of nowhere, giants, trolls, goblins, demons, humans, holograms, and avatars appeared.

"Um, Michael?" John said.

"Yes?"

"It was said that when we needed them, there would be angels here to help, right?"

"Yes, that is correct" Michael said.

"I think we need them now."

"Call upon them," he said.

John took a breath and closed his eyes.

"I call upon the angels of the Most High God!" John yelled in a loud voice.

"Help us in our time of need!"

"John?" Sarah said.

John opened his eyes and looked at Sarah, who was looking behind her.

"I think the reinforcements have arrived."

John turned his head to get a better look and gasped.

"This must be how Elisha's servant felt in 1st or 2nd Kings," John said.

"2nd Kings," Michael said. "Chapter 6."

"I enjoyed that moment," Theron added.

"It's like we have all the angels of Heaven here!"

"Not even close," Theron said.

Stone swore.

"They were not supposed to have this much help!"

Trisha looked amazed as she saw the multitudes on both sides.

"We can win, right?" Trisha asked.

Stone didn't even look at her, all he said was, "Attack!"

CHAPTER EIGHTEEN

The four adults stared at the computer screen in astonishment.

"Lord, have mercy!" Jack said.

"We need to pray," Pastor Stevens said. "Maggie shut the monitor off."

"But--" Maggie started to say.

"We can't do anything by watching them, we can by praying for them. The battle must first be fought spiritually on our knees in prayer before the victory will manifest in the natural," Pastor Stevens explained.

Maggie nodded and shut the monitor off.

She turned her chair, and they faced each other in a circle and prayed.

Liz stood, Bobby beside her.

"So, this is what it comes down to," she said.

"Yes," Bobby said.

"The other battles were nothing compared to this," Liz said.

"The Lord is still in control. You know that, don't you?"

Liz rubbed her arms.

"Yes, I know. It's just, I've never seen anything like this before."

"You walk by faith, not by sight."

"You're right," Liz said.

Liz knelt down and started praying.

Bobby joined her once more.

Deli pulled out her staff, tossed it to Trisha, and said, "Here you go kid. Go have some fun."

Trisha caught the staff.

"Thanks," she said. "Come on, Airborne!"

As the unicorn started running, he asked, *Land or air?*

Trisha thought for a second. "Land!" she yelled out.

As you wish.

The unicorn continued to run.

Tim was able to fire upon a half dozen creatures before any of them could reach him or his friends.

"Keep away from those huge skunks!" he said.

"My scans show that they have a gas that'll knock you out!"

"We'll take care of those," Theron said. "And the demons, as well."

As Ashley was taking aim at the fast-approaching trolls coming at her, she didn't notice the girl with the rainbow-horned unicorn riding toward her holding a staff.

"Ashley! Look out!" Tim yelled, firing his laser at her attacker.

The laser beam went through, seemingly unnoticed by the rider.

The girl swung her staff at Ashley, connecting with her mid-section.

"Ugh!" Ashley cried, falling off her unicorn.

As she hit the ground, Ashley accidentally fired off an arrow.

"No!" Ashley said as she saw the arrow heading for Sarah's back.

The arrow passed through and hit the goblin Sarah was fighting.

The goblin fell and Sarah turned around, unharmed.

"Oh, thank You, God," Ashley said as she rolled to a standing position.

Sarah dismounted her unicorn and ran over to Ashley.

Tim did as well.

"You're okay..." Ashley said, breathless.

"What happened?" Sarah asked. "That tickled."

"Really? It did?" Ashley asked.

"I think," Tim said, turning his back and firing at anything that moved, "thankfully, our weapons don't hurt real people. That girl who hit you, Ash, was human. I didn't pay attention to my scanner when I saw you were in trouble. I fired and nothing happened. Are you okay?"

"Just a little winded," Ashley said, rubbing her stomach. "That's all. I'll be ok."

"Good," Tim said. "Let's get back to it so we can grab Jess and get out of here."

"Agreed," Ashley said. "Let's move out!"

Tim's jet pack fired up and he took to the air.

He fired at oversized bats, skeletal creatures with wings, pterodactyls, and even what appeared to be a flying stingray with an electronic barb.

"Unbelievable!" Tim said.

John and Plate, who had long since dismounted their unicorns, were now fighting a one and a half-story giant holding a huge club.

"You go right, I'll go left," John said. "Maybe we can find an opening."

"Sounds good!" Plate said.

As the giant brought its club down, John and Plate spread out.

John ran closer to the giant, using his spiked shield to come down hard on its foot.

The giant roared as sparks flew from its foot.

"Good news!" John yelled to Plate. "This thing is a robot!"

"Good," Plate said as he used his laser sword to cut the giant's back heel.

More sparks flew.

The giant roared louder.

Plate grabbed his other sword and attacked the giant's back legs before it could move.

The giant fell to its knees.

John and Plate both looked at each other and ran up its legs. They both ran up to the giant's head, hitting its back with their swords as they went, sparks flying everywhere.

"ARGH!!" the giant yelled.

"They love exaggeration," John spoke out loud.

When they reached the head, Plate turned one of his swords back into a whip, on the highest setting, and started whipping at its head.

The giant tried to swat at them like a fly, but Plate was careful to avoid the attack.

John was hit with its hand and fell.

"John!" Plate yelled, sparks flying all around him.

The giant's big hand went up like it was going to smash John like a bug.

John rolled away, as the hand came down, narrowly escaping being crushed underneath.

"Get back!" John heard Plate yell, "It's gonna blow!"

John saw Plate jump off the giant and start running toward him.

"Go, go, go!" Plate yelled.

Without warning, John and Plate were both knocked to the ground and covered.

They heard an explosion.

The covering that had protected them lifted.

"Are you two alright?" they heard a voice ask.

John and Plate looked up into the face of one of the angels.

"Uh, yeah," Plate said, rubbing the back of his neck.

"But I think we should leave the giant robots for you guys to handle."

"Right away!" The angel said as he took flight and left.

As he got up, Plate picked up his laser swords and latched one of them back onto his belt.

"Well," Plate said, offering his hand to John.

"It looks like the giants will be taken care of, huh?"

John accepted his hand and stood.

"Looks that way," he said. "Now, let's go fight something our own size!"

"Or smaller," Plate said.

Just before she knocked the girl off her unicorn, Trisha felt a tickle.

It wasn't until she had hit the girl with her staff and was away that she thought about it.

What was that? she thought.

She didn't think long about it as she swung her staff at a couple of people who looked like animal-faced monks.

They are ugly on both sides, Trisha though.

"Fly us back!" Trisha yelled. "I've had enough for now."

As you wish, Airborne said, flapping his wings and taking to the air.

This is just crazy, she thought as she flew back.

When she got back, she noticed Stone and Deli still hadn't moved.

When she landed, Deli asked, "Back so soon?"

"I decided to take a little break," Trisha said, handing the staff back to Deli.

"Keep it," Deli said, "I'm sure you're not finished with it just yet."

As Tim fired upon the flying beasts, he noticed that the number of demons were dwindling.

Some retreated while others were hit and vanished in a black cloud.

"Thank you, Lord," Tim prayed out loud.

John and Plate fought side by side, fighting the trolls, goblins, robots, and other creatures that came their way.

"I think," Plate said, swinging his whip, "I like facing the ones that just disappear when you defeat them. It's just easier to walk away."

"I know what you mean," John said, dodging a zombie with hooks for hands.

"This looked much easier in Lord of the Rings, I gotta tell ya!" Plate said, swinging a troll into the zombie fighting with John.

"Yeah, but that journey took place over three months or so!" John replied, swinging his sword into the chest of a goblin coming at him.

"They didn't get back to the shire until a year had passed!"

"Okay, so maybe it wasn't that easy!" Plate said, continuing to fight.

Sarah and Ashley were on one unicorn, riding fast.

Ashley was in front firing her arrows at anything that was in their way.

Sarah was in the back, cutting down anything that wouldn't go down with Ashley's arrows.

Suddenly, a demon landed in front of them.

The unicorn stopped.

The demon outstretched its wings, sulfur rising from his nostrils.

"My, my, my," the demon spoke. "What have we here?"

"Two servants of the Almighty God!" Sarah said without hesitation.

The demon gave a murderous look.

"Ah, yes," the demon said. "Servants of the Imposter!"

"Bite your tongue, demon!" Ashley yelled.

The demon grabbed Ashley by her hood.

"Hey!" Ashley yelled.

"Unhand her!" Sarah shouted.

The demon laughed.

"And who's going to make me? You?"

"Up!" Sarah yelled to the Unicorn.

The unicorn flew toward the demon, and Sarah tried to hit him with her sword.

Sarah was knocked off her unicorn and hit the ground.

The demon laughed.

"Pathetic humans! Do you think your little weapons will hurt me?"

"The Lord Jesus rebuke thee!"

The demon flinched and dropped Ashley.

"How dare you use that Name!" the demon screamed.

"In the Name of Jesus," Ashley yelled, standing up, "you have no power against us!"

Rage could be seen in the demon's eyes.

"Shut up! That Name means nothing here!"

"In the Name of Jesus, return to the pits of Hell!"

The demon went down to his knees and screamed an unearthly scream and fell on his face.

Then the demon laughed an unholy laugh.

"Foolish children!" he said, raising his head, laughing.

"I have never been to the pits of Hell! How, then shall I return?"

The demon roared with laughter.

Sarah and Ashley looked at each other.

Then Ashley said, "By the authority and power of Jesus, my Lord, and Savior, I command you, demon, to leave us and depart into the innermost parts of Hell, never to be seen again!"

The demon grabbed his head and screamed, "NO!!!! You have no power here! No right!"

"In the Name of Jesus, be gone!" Sarah said.

The demon left in a cloud of smoke and sulfur, his screams echoing.

Sarah and Ashley hugged.

"Oh, thank God that's over!" Ashley said.

"Yeah, I-" Sarah stopped herself. "Oh, no!"

"What?" Ashley asked, looking in the same direction as Sarah.

Ashley gasped.

The unicorn lay on the ground, its horn broken, and its right front leg at an awkward angle.

Sarah and Ashley rushed to the unicorn's side.

The unicorn was barely breathing.

"Oh, God, no," Sarah prayed.

"Should we-" Ashley started, holding back tears. "Should we put it down?"

"Help me fix the leg," Sarah said, ignoring the question.

"Sarah-"

"Just help me, okay?" Tears forming in Sarah's eyes.

Slowly, they both worked at setting the leg back in place.

The unicorn raised its head and gave a slight horse's neigh.

"Shh, shh," Sarah said, putting her hand on its head.

"We're trying to help."

The unicorn laid its head back down.

"Lord," Sarah closed her eyes to pray, "please, I beg You, stop this poor creature's pain. I don't want to put it down, Lord. I don't even know if this creature matters much because it exists in this world. Heal it, Lord, or let it go fast. I pray, in Jesus' Name, Amen."

"Amen," Ashley repeated.

Sarah's hands began to feel warm.

She opened her eyes and gasped.

One hand was on the unicorn's head and the other on its leg, and they were glowing!

"Ashley!" Sarah said.

"I see it!" Ashley replied.

Sarah and Ashley both watched in awe as they saw the horn heal back into one piece and the leg snapped back into place.

"Oh, thank You, Lord!" Sarah yelled.

The unicorn immediately stood up.

"Are you done yet?" A voice said.

Sarah and Ashley looked behind them.

Theron stood guard, watching.

"How long have you been there?" Sarah asked.

"Ever since you went to the aide of your unicorn," he said, smiling.

"Someone had to watch your back."

"Thanks," Ashley said.

"Not a problem. Are you ready to fight again?"

"We sure are," Sarah said, petting the unicorn's mane.

"Good," Theron said. "Let's get going."

CHAPTER NINETEEN

After taking out most of the air creatures, Tim was about to get to the ground when he heard a voice from above.

"We meet again, I see!"

Before he could look up, Tim's arms were grabbed by strong claws.

"What?" Tim yelled.

"Have you thought any more about my offer?"

"Satan!" Tim yelled, "let go of me!"

"You do know you will lose this battle, don't you? You only have two avatar buddies left. That leaves seven of you and I'm sure all of you can be dealt with easily. I might just spare you all if you just take my deal."

"In case you didn't notice, Satan, your numbers are dwindling, too. You're no match for these angels!"

Satan laughed.

"I don't have to deal with the angels. Once I deal with you and your friends, the angels won't have any reason to stick around!"

"Let go of me!" Tim yelled.

"Will you take my deal so I might spare you and your friends' lives, or will I have to crush you?"

"The Lord rebuke you!"

Satan screamed.

"If that's how you want it," Satan said, grabbing Tim with his tail, "fine!"

Satan hurled Tim with his powerful tail and then disappeared.

The last thing Tim remembered before he lost consciousness was flying through a window, crashing through glass, and hitting a wall.

"Trish!"

Trisha turned around and saw Travis running out of the fortress, running toward her.

"Trish!" Travis said, taking a breath. "Most of the creatures here have all been destroyed! All the land and most of the air creatures have been destroyed, except for all the unicorns and a red dragon."

Trisha looked up in the sky. "Red dragon?" she asked.

"I don't see a red dragon."

"It comes and goes," Travis said. "Unlike the others. I've seen it appear and disappear a few times."

Weird, she thought. *Then again, what isn't?*

"I have to tell you," he continued with a laugh, "that this place is far out!"

"Get everyone out here," Trisha said. "It's time we finished what we started in the alley."

"Yeah, sure," Travis said. "No problem."

Travis ran back in to gather the rest.

Trisha surveyed the damage around her.

Robotic bodies everywhere sparking, demons fleeing while others disappeared in clouds of smoke.

Weren't we supposed to win this battle? she thought.

Stone walked over to her and said, "You look disappointed."

Trisha turned to look at him. "I thought we were supposed to win."

"Who says we haven't?" Stone replied.

"I don't understand," Trisha said, confused.

"The main battle is with Jessica. Even as we speak, she is being tormented in her nightmares. The original plan for this was just to break her will and have her reject her faith. This battle was just an added bonus."

"I still don't get it," Trisha said.

"The way it was supposed to go was Jessica's faced all this," Stone said waving his hand around.

"You, me, and every other creature in between. But this worked out so much better. She is stuck in a nightmare far worse than this, and we get to punish her friends as well."

Trisha thought a moment.

"I think I understand now," she said.

"Good," Stone said.

"Ashley?" Sarah asked, riding her unicorn.

"Yeah," Ashley answered, walking alongside her.

"You know when you and Tim were talking about the water?"

"Yeah?"

"Well, there are some things over there, and they are coming out!"

Ashley stopped walking to let Sarah's unicorn pass so she could see.

"Great," she said. "If all those other creepy creatures weren't enough, we have Swamp Thing coming after us!"

"I thought Swamp Thing was a good guy," Sarah said.

"That's not the point, Sarah!"

Out of the water came a humanoid shape of seaweed.

"Seaweed?" Sarah asked. "What's next? Corel reef?"

As if to answer her question, a humanoid Corel reef walked out of the water.

"I was just joking!" Sarah said. "That's it! I think I need to keep my mouth shut."

Ashley raised her crossbows and fired.

The arrows hit Seaweed in the head, passing through and hitting Corel Reef. Seaweed popped like a water balloon, but Corel Reef kept walking. Ashley looked at Sarah, who was dismounting her unicorn.

"What do you say?" she asked. "I take Seaweeds and you take Corel Reef?"

"Sounds good."

Ashley then looked at Theron.

"And could you take everything else in between?"

"That I can do," Theron said.

Ashley fired off more rounds as Sarah worked on the Corel Reef and Theron cut down anything else that came out of the water. When Corel Reefs were hit by Sarah's sword, they shattered into hundreds of pieces. Sarah's unicorn joined in, stomping on some and maiming others with his horn. Ashley kept firing. Within minutes of fighting, nothing else crawled out from the water.

"Is that it?" Ashley asked.

"You want more?" Sarah asked.

"No, thank you!"

"Good," Sarah said, mounting her unicorn. "Get on and let's go."

Sarah extended her arm out to Ashley and pulled her up.

"Ready?" she asked.

"Yeah."

"Are you coming, Theron?" Sarah asked.

"Lead the way," Theron replied.

———

For what felt like forever, John and Plate, with the help of a few angels, finally defeated the last of the remaining goblins and company.

"Is that the last of them?" John asked, resting on his sword.

"All except the demons, but they are being taken care of by the other angels," an angel said.

"And, of course, those in and around the fortress."

"What's over there?" John asked, not even bothering to look.

"Just Stone, another demon named Infidelity, the cult he has brought with him, and a few avatars."

"That helps," John said, "How many in all?"

"Just over thirty," the angel replied.

John let out a groan.

"Speaking of which," Plate said as Sarah and Ashley came riding up to them, "Where's our avatars?"

"Right here," Tank said, walking alongside J9M.

"We are all that's left," J9M said, "barely."

"A couple more hits like the ones we just faced, and we'll be no use to ya'll."

"Well then," John said, "don't get hit."

"Easier said than done, kid," Tank replied.

John walked over to the girls on the unicorn.

"Are you two okay?" he asked, rubbing the unicorn's mane.

"Just fine," Sarah said.

The unicorn's eyes met John's.

Tell Miss Sarah "Thank you" for healing me.

"Sarah?" John said, still looking at the unicorn.

"Yeah?"

"This unicorn says thank you for healing him," he said.

He looked up at her and asked, "What happened?"

"Well, uh, um, his leg was broken, and so was his horn," she explained, blushing.

"I just prayed for his healing."

John looked at the unicorn's leg and horn.

We fell, attacking a demon. I fell hard. Your God has blessed her with healing hands.

John paled and looked up at Sarah. "You fought a demon?"

"I wouldn't say fought, per se," Sarah said.

"More like rebuked it and sent it to the Abyss."

"He told me," John said, motioning to the unicorn, "that you attacked a demon."

"The demon had grabbed Ashley and, yes, I tried to attack the demon. That's how he got hurt."

Plate looked at Ashley.

"Are you okay?" he asked.

"Yes, Plate," Ashley said. "I'm fine."

John shook his head.

"Anyway, he says that God has blessed you with healing hands."

Sarah smiled and rubbed it's head.

"Thanks," she whispered in the unicorn's ear.

"Hey," J9M said. "If you can heal a unicorn, can you restore a couple of avatars' energy? I want to continue the fight!"

"Yeah," Tank said. "I want to accomplish this mission, to make sure this place is shut down."

"I don't know," Sarah said, a little uneasy.

"Hey," J9M said, "the worst thing that could happen is nothing at all, am I right?"

Sarah looked at John and asked, "Should I try it?"

"It wouldn't hurt anything," Michael said, landing with Theron beside him.

Looking at the other angel, Michael said, "Carry on, Joel."

"Yes, my Captain," the angel named Joel said, taking flight and joining the other angels in battle.

Michael turned his attention back to Sarah.

"You have been granted a unique gift from The Most High. Use it for His glory."

"You mean," Sarah said slowly, "I really have a gift of healing?"

"To honor and glorify the Lord with it, yes."

"But how does healing a unicorn in this world bring Him honor?" Sarah asked.

"The Almighty cares about what you care about," Michael explained. "When it broke your heart to see this noble creature in pain, He revealed this gift to you. You, calling out to Him for the mercy of this creature gave honor to Him."

"Oh," she said.

"Are you ready to once again use your gift?"

"Yes," Sarah said, dismounting her unicorn.

She walked over to the only two remaining avatars and placed a hand on each of them.

She took a breath, looked around, and said, "Pray with me, please."

Everyone bowed their heads.

"Lord," Sarah prayed, "I come to You and humbly ask that You heal these two that are before me. Not just to restore the energy to their avatars, but to touch them physically, Lord. Whatever issues they have, Lord, I pray You would heal them, so it'll glorify You. Amen."

"Amen," the gathered group said.

When they looked up, they saw a glow around Sarah's hands, then it was gone. Sarah took her hands off the two and said, "So? Anything?"

"Whoa!" J9M said, "My energy meter is off the scale!"

"Mine, too," Tank said. "Thanks for the request on our real bodies, I won't know if it's been done until I get out of the pod I'm in."

Sarah smiled and turned to J9M. "What about you? Feel any different at home?"

"Uh, yeah, but I'd rather not talk about it right now. If you don't mind."

"Oh. Sure, no problem," Sarah said.

"Hey, where's Tim?" Ashley asked, looking around.

"I haven't seen him in a while."

"He had another bout with Lucifer in the air," Theron said.

"He was thrown into Jessica's room."

Fear filled Ashley's face as she asked, "Is he okay?"

"For the moment, yes."

"Thank God," she said, relieved.

"I say it's time to storm the fortress," Plate said.

"But first we have to get past the doors," John said.

"Joel was right, just over thirty are over there."

"Let's not keep them waiting, then," Plate said.

"Trisha," Stone said, "You and the rest take the six in front, Deli and I will handle the other two."

"Got it," Trisha said. "Should we attack now, or wait?"

Stone was quiet for a moment.

Just when she thought she might have to ask again, he spoke.

"Now would be a good time; they are close enough."

Trisha nodded.

"Attack!" she cried.

CHAPTER TWENTY

Tim groaned.

"Ah, you're alive, I see," Tim heard a young, female voice say.

Tim opened his eyes and saw a young girl between ten and thirteen years old standing over him.

"A remedy I'm sure I can fix!" The girl said.

The girl grabbed him by the suit and threw him across the room.

"Ugh!" Tim cried out as he hit another wall.

What strength! Tim thought as he stood and took in his surroundings.

He saw what looked to be a bathroom and a figure lying on a cot, some sort of goggles on the person's face.

Tim sucked in a breath. "Jess?"

"She can't hear you right now," the girl said. "She's rather busy."

"What have you done to her?" he demanded.

"Oh, a little of this, a little of that," she said.

As the girl advanced forward, he scanned her.

Demon possessed? Tim thought as he read the readout.

Oh, great! He thought with a groan.

"But it is nothing compared to what I am going to do to you!" she said as she lunged toward him.

"The Lord rebuke you!" Tim yelled.

The demon-possessed girl screamed and stumbled back.

"You will pay for that!" she screamed, rage in her eyes.

Tim didn't miss a beat. "In the name of Jesus, I command you to come out of her, you unclean spirit!"

The girl gave a guttural cry. "She invited me in! Mind your own business!"

"In the name of Christ, let me talk with her!"

"No!" the girl yelled again.

"In the name of Jesus Christ, demon, let me talk to her!"

The girl fell to her knees.

"Let me talk to her, demon, in the name of Christ!"

The girl looked up and Tim could see clarity in her eyes.

"Help me!" the girl screamed.

"Come out of her, you dark spirit!"

The girl's eyes clouded over and the demon within her said, "Never! She is mine! I'm not done with her!"

Again, Tim yelled, "Come out of her now, dark one, in the name of Jesus Christ!"

The girl screamed again. "No!"

"In the name of Jesus Christ, I command you to leave her! Come out of her now!"

A mighty wind knocked Tim down, dazing him.

Tim looked, and standing in front of him was a large demon, hate in its eyes.

Tim looked over and saw the little girl lying on the ground.

"You wanted me out," the demon roared. "Well, here I am!"

For the first time in hours, Kim was free of the demon, Bal'ack.

Oh, thank You, God, she prayed. *Forgive me, Lord. Be my God and save my soul. Save me, Jesus.*

She then heard a monstrous voice.

"You wanted me out! Well, here I am!"

"Bal'ack," Kim whispered, looking for a place to hide.

She noticed the bathroom.

She tried to think.

Wasn't there something said about the bathroom being a sanctuary?

Yes!

Jessica went in there to get away from the holographic images!

"What are you going to do now, you puny human?" Bal'ack screamed.

Kim tried to slowly crawl to the bathroom, hoping the demon would be distracted by the person in the battle suit.

Lord, protect him, she prayed.

"Where do you think you are going?" she heard Bal' ack say.

She looked over and the demon was looking right at her!

The demon grabbed her by the collar and lifted her up.

"Remember what I told you before, Kim," Bal'ack said.

"Bal'ack!" Kim pleaded, "Please, don't!"

Bal'ack laughed. "I said I'd let you go, and I intend to keep my word."

"Please," Kim said, "Don't!"

"Too late!" he said with a laugh as he threw her out the window.

As Kim flew out the window, she didn't feel fear, but peace.

"No!" Tim cried as he saw the girl, Kim, get tossed out the window like a rag doll.

The demon named Bal'ack turned to Tim and laughed. "You are next, young fool!" he said, picking Tim up and throwing him against the wall. "Only much more slowly!"

Tim hit the wall with a pounding thud.

"God, help me," Tim prayed as he rolled unto his side and saw Bal'ack just standing there.

His strength should have already killed me! Tim thought.

"Come on, you puny human!" the demon shouted. "Stand so I can crush you!"

"I can do all things through Christ who gives me the strength," Tim whispered.

You are protected in My Love. I am with you, always.

"Yes, Lord, thank You," Tim prayed as he stood. He then said to Bal'ack, "You will not touch me!"

Bal'ack laughed. "I will do what I want!" the demon shouted.

"In the name of Christ, you are through!"

Bal'ack stumbled back.

"I curse you and your God," he said, mixing God's name with profanities.

"You will not use my Lord's name that way!" Tim yelled. "In the name of Jesus Christ, I bind you!"

Out of nowhere, chains appeared around Bal'ack, binding him.

Um, okay, Tim thought, astonished that actual chains materialized.

Bal'ack fell to the ground, roaring. "Let go of me! You have no power!"

"The power comes from Christ!" Tim yelled.

"In the name of Jesus Christ, I cast you into the pit of darkness!"

"No!" The demon yelled. "You can't do this!"

"Begone, you foul spirit! In the name of Jesus Christ!"

"No!" The demon's voice echoed as he vanished in a cloud of smoke.

Tim fell to his knees and thanked God. "Oh, God, thank You for the words."

Tim lifted his head, walked over to the window, and looked down.

He saw what looked like the girl that had knocked Ashley off her unicorn, kneeling over the girl, Kim, crying. Two others were standing over her. It was Stone and someone else.

The girl looked up at him and yelled, "You! You killed her! You killed my sister!"

Suddenly, behind him, Tim heard a fearful scream.

Tim turned around and saw Jessica sitting up, panicking and trying to remove the goggles off her head.

"Jess!"

"Michael!" Stone said swinging a sword at him. "How very nice to see you again!"

"Stonewraith!" Michael said, drawing out his own sword in a countermove.

"Good to see you remember me," Stone said. "Even if I am wearing someone else's flesh."

"You have lost this battle," Michael said.

"Lost?" Stone said. "I think not!"

Stone swung his sword and Michael countered.

"You should join us, Michael," Stone said. "You would be an excellent addition."

"Never, traitor!" Michael said. "I will not share in your judgment of the lake of fire!"

"Lake of fire! Ha!" Stone laughed. "If that place existed, He would have sent us there by now! But no! He is not as powerful as He wants you to believe. You! Michael, you should have found out the truth by now! He is a fraud!"

"Bite your tongue, demon! You will not talk about the Almighty in that way!"

Stone heard a loud roar come from the fortress.

"Looks like it's time for me to go," Stone said, retreating.

Michael put his sword away and watched as Stone ran away.

———

"Theron," Deli said, swinging her bow, "Long time, no see!"

"Not long enough, Infidelity!" Theron said, dodging her attacks.

"What," she said, looking hurt, "you aren't happy to see an old friend?"

"I'd be happy to see you if you had never changed loyalties and were fighting by my side!"

"You're gonna let that come between our friendship?"

Deli asked, aiming for his head.

"I will not have fellowship with darkness!" Theron yelled.

"Have it your way!"

Deli swung her bow, connecting a couple of times with Theron's legs.

"Ugh!"

"Had enough?" Deli asked.

"Not on your life!" Theron said.

"Have it your way!" Again, she swung her bow.

Theron's sword connected with it, and it flew out of her hands.

"Bravo," Deli said. "I guess this is where I take leave."

Deli retreated from Theron, picking up her bow in the process.

"We'll have to do this again sometime," Deli said, turning around and blowing him a kiss.

"Right," Theron said.

After fighting for a while, Trisha got off her unicorn, hoping to fight more effectively.

The more she fought, the more people she lost, their avatars vanishing, while the other side lost no one.

Oh, come on! she thought. *Something's got to give.*

"Your fighting's rather clumsy," the avatar said.

"Shut up!" she said, swinging her staff.

"I'm sure if you took lessons, you could improve," he said, dodging her attacks.

"Be quiet, you stupid avatar!" Trisha yelled.

"Stupid?" the avatar said. "I'll have you know, I was a straight-A student in school."

"Good for you!" Trisha said through clenched teeth, swinging wildly.

"Tell me," he said, defending himself, never attacking.

"How are your grades? You're still in High school, right?"

"Shut up and fight," Trisha yelled.

"Sorry, I've been told you're a human. I don't wanna hurt you."

"How touching," Trisha yelled, getting tired of all the banter.

"Save the chivalry for someone else."

Suddenly, Trisha heard an unearthly roar echoing from the fortress.

Trisha backed up from the fight. The avatar did the same, seemingly occupied by the noise, as well.

What was that? Trisha thought. *It sounded like it came from up in the room where Jessica was.*

"Kim!" Trisha said, running toward the fortress, the battle was forgotten.

I hope she's okay!

Before she could take another few steps, she saw someone flying out the window.

Trisha's heart skipped a beat.

"Kim!" she screamed. "No!"

Oh, please, no! Trisha though, frozen in place.

The world seemed to move in slow motion as she watched her little sister fall to her death.

Kim fell to the ground and bounced two or three feet in the air before she finally landed.

"Kim!" Trisha yelled, running as fast as she could to her fallen sister.

When she reached her, Trisha fell to her knees.

"Kim?" Trisha said.

Kim didn't move, her body was lifeless.

"Trisha," she heard Stone's voice say.

Trisha looked over and saw Deli and Stone standing to the side, watching.

"She's dead!" Trisha cried. "She's dead and it's all my fault. I never should have brought her here!"

Stone said nothing.

"Kim!" she said once more.

"Oh, God, I never should have brought her here," she said as she looked up.

She looked at the window where Kim had fallen and saw someone.

Though he was wearing a helmet, and was at a great distance, she knew who it was that was standing there.

He's one of her friends, Trisha thought, referring to Jessica.

"You!" She yelled up at him. "You killed her! You killed my sister!"

The young man stepped away from the window, but Trisha continued to scream.

"I hate you! You will pay for what you have done!"

Trisha closed her eyes and sobbed.

Stone came over and lifted Kim's lifeless body.

"Deli," Stone said, "grab Trisha, and let's go."

"The rest of you," Stone said to the others that started to gather around Trisha, "Let's go."

Trisha didn't put up a fight as Deli lifted her over her shoulder.

She's dead, Trisha thought. *What am I gonna do now?*

What am I gonna tell Mom?

John watched as Stone lifted Kim's lifeless body and gave some orders.

Stone then looked at their little group and said, "This isn't over! Tell Ronald I plan on seeing him again!"

John raised his sword and was about to charge when Michael spoke. "No, let them leave."

"But—"John started to protest.

"They are retreating. Jessica has been rescued," Michael said.

"Yes, sir," John said.

CHAPTER TWENTY-ONE

Jessica's screams wouldn't stop as she futilely tried to take the goggles off.

"Jess! Jessica, hold still!" Tim said, also trying to remove the goggles.

It didn't seem like she heard anything except her own screams.

Finally, Tim was able to remove them.

Jess continued to scream even after the goggles were removed.

She was drenched in sweat.

"Jess!" Tim said, putting his hands on her shoulders.

Jessica faced him and started screaming and crying. "Don't hurt me, again!" she pleaded, "Please, I beg you!"

"What?" Tim asked, confused.

Then he realized she wasn't seeing him.

My helmet, she doesn't recognize me!

Without a second thought, Tim ripped his helmet off, revealing his face. "Jess!" he said, "It's me, Tim!"

Something in Jessica's eyes registered.

"Tim?" she asked, unsure.

He moved the hair from out of her face and said, "Yeah, Jess. It's me."

Jessica cried as she wrapped her arms around him. "Oh, Tim! It was real! So very, very real!"

"I've got you," Tim said.

Tim held Jessica as she cried.

He had no idea how long they were like that when he heard what sounded like glass breaking.

Tim looked over; arm out ready to blast anything unfriendly.

"Whoa. Easy there," John said, walking over, and stepping on more broken glass in the process. "We come in peace."

Tim lowered his arm. "How'd we make out?"

"We lost all our avatar friends except J9M and Tank," John replied. "Right now, they are trying to close the internet link. Theron is back there with them."

"The girl," Tim asked. "She's dead, isn't she?"

"Yes," Michael said, walking in, the others joining him. "But, not without finding the Lord first."

"Thank God," Tim said, his eyes watering. "She...she was possessed. When I commanded the demon to come out of her, he did. He then threw her out the window. There wasn't anything I could do."

"That's horrible," John said.

"How's Jess?" Sarah asked, walking over.

"I think she cried herself to sleep," Tim said.

"She was unconscious, wearing that thing."

Tim directed his attention to the goggles on the floor.

"What was it for?" Plate said, picking it up.

"I have no idea," Tim said.

"Come," Michael said, "Let's get going."

Michael stepped up to Tim and said, "Here, let me carry her."

Tim moved and let the archangel lift Jessica up.

They left the room and walked to where the two avatars were, trying to disable the internet link.

"The link is closed," Theron said.

"What?" Tank asked. "How can that be, we haven't found it yet."

"Yeah," J9M said. "We're still here as if you couldn't tell."

"You are still here because you were allowed to remain," Theron said.

215

"Given what has happened," Tank said. "That makes sense, sort of."

"Hey," J9M said, noticing Michael and the rest. "Is that the Shining King's Daughter?"

Michael looked at the avatar. "Yes," he said. "This is Jessica."

"I guess...it's over," J9M said.

Michael said nothing.

"Hey, uh, look," J9M said to John. "It was nice working with ya, given the circumstances, I mean."

"Yes," John said, extending his hand, "Thank you for all your help."

J9M took John's hand and shook it. "Glad to be of service."

"Thank you too, Tank," he said offering his hand as well.

"No problem," Tank said, taking John's hand. "It's what we do."

"Anyway," J9M said, "I'd like to keep in contact with you guys, that is if you don't mind."

John smiled.

"I think we'd like that."

"Great," J9M said, giving John his e-mail address.

"Thanks," John said. "I'm sure I'll remember it."

"Great," J9M said.

Looking around, he asked, "So, ah, how do we get out of here?"

"This door," Theron said, opening up a hidden door.

"Where did that come from?" J9M asked.

"Don't ask," Tim said. "It's less to think about."

"Good point," J9M said.

"So," Tank said. "When we go through the door, we all go back to our respective places, right?"

"Yes," Theron said. "That is how it will work."

"Well, then," Tank said. "I guess this is it. I might see you guys on the other side. Tell Jack to be expecting a phone call from me."

"What?" John asked. "You know Jack? Jack Pippirelli? How's that?"

"That'll have to wait for another day," Tank said as he stepped through the door first and disappeared.

"Well," J9M said. "I guess it's my turn now, huh?"

He stepped through the door and was gone.

"Alright, guys," John said. "Let's go."

As everyone walked through the door, John looked out the window and saw the unicorn, Gemstone.

Their eyes locked.

Your God has blessed you and your friends with gifts. Use them to glorify Him.

John nodded.

The unicorn faded away as he stepped through the door.

CHAPTER TWENTY-TWO

Liz opened her eyes and found herself staring up into the eyes of Bobby, still in his angel form.

"Welcome back," Bobby said.

Liz sat up and lowered her legs to the floor. "We're back?" Liz asked.

"Yes."

"What about Jessica? And the kids?"

"They are on their way."

"Thank God!"

"Indeed."

Liz stood. "Jack?" Liz asked as she walked to the door frame. "Oh," she caught herself.

Jack, Maggie, and Pastor were in a circle praying.

They must have heard a noise because they all looked up and noticed her.

"Liz?" Jack stood. "Are you okay?"

"I'm fine."

Jack looked behind Liz.

"Bobby?" he asked.

"Yes, sir, it's me."

"Well, I'll be," Pastor Stevens said, rising from his chair.

"For we have entertained angels unaware."

"Yes, you have," Bobby said.

"Maggie," Jack said, "turn on the monitor, I want to know what's happening with the kids."

Maggie turned on the monitor to find a black screen.

"It appears to be offline," Maggie said.

"That must mean the kids did it!" Jack said.

"Yes, they did," Bobby said.

Just then, the door opened, and out stepped Plate, Ashley, Sarah, Tim, Theron, Michael, and John.

Michael was holding Jessica in his arms.

"Jessica!" Liz exclaimed.

"Here, put her on the cot out here," she said directing the angel out of the room to the cot.

Everyone followed Michael out of the room and watched him place Jessica on the cot.

Liz knelt down and stroked her daughter's cheek.

"Oh, Jess, honey," Liz said.

Jessica's eyes flew open, and a tiny scream came from her mouth.

She looked around and then at her mom's face.

"Mom?" Jess said. "Oh, Mom!" she said, wrapping her arms around her mother's neck.

Liz held Jessica and sat on the cot.

Jessica sobbed.

"Everything's fine now. It'll be okay. It's over."

"It's not over!" Jessica said through sobs.

Satan stood at the Throne of God once again.

"I'm not done with Jessica or her friends just yet!" Satan yelled. "I want that town back once more!"

"I will think upon your request, Satan!" the voice of God boomed. "I will answer you at another time!"

"Fine!" Satan said. "I'll be back!"

Satan left in a rage.

"Bring her in," God said to Avdeel.

"Yes, my Lord," Avdeel replied.

A young girl stepped in front of the Throne of God.

"Kimberly Anne Conner," God's voice spoke in love. "A mansion has been prepared for you in My house. Welcome, My dear child."

Kim knelt down. "Thank you, my Lord and my God."

———

Satan surveyed the damage.

The two-way mirror shattered.

He walked over to the console, glass crunching underneath his feet.

He pressed a few buttons, and the monitors came to life.

"Perfect," he said.

He touched a few more buttons and two different recordings started playing.

"Just like Stone said," Satan mused. "Beautiful! Absolutely beautiful!"

EPILOGUE

911 Operator: "911. What seems to be the emergency?"

Caller: "Yeah, uh, I just saw a little girl get hit by a hit-and-run driver!"

(Screams in the background)

911 Operator: "Can you tell if the victim is alive and breathing?"

(Girl in the background: "Kim!")

Caller: "I don't know! It happened so fast! The car hit her, and she just went flying!"

911 Operator: "Where are you at, sir?"

Caller: "Um...I'm not from around here! I don't see any street signs!"

911 Operator: "Okay, sir. Stay calm. Are there any buildings or other landmarks around you?"

(Screaming continues)

Caller: "Uh, Railroad tracks! I see railroad tracks."

911 Operator: "Okay, anything else?"

Caller: "Yeah, um, Jeff's Stock, it's a grocery store, I think."

911 Operator: "That's good. I know where you are. Help is on the way."

(Girl in the background: "Kim! Don't leave me!")

Caller: "Oh, Thank you!"

911 Operator: "I'm going to need your name, sir."

(Background: "Kim!")

Caller: "My name's Stone."

911 Operator: "Okay, Mr. Stone, stay on the line until help arrives..."

www.ingramcontent.com/pod-product-compliance
Lightning Source LLC
Chambersburg PA
CBHW061456030726
47503CB00005B/1731